7.00

THE DISTANT
LOVER

CHRISTOPH HEIN

. . . .

THE DISTANT LOVER

TRANSLATED FROM THE GERMAN
BY KRISHNA WINSTON

PANTHEON BOOKS   NEW YORK

All rights reserved under International and Pan-American Copyright Conventions. Published in the United States by Pantheon Books, a division of Random House, Inc., New York, and simultaneously in Canada by Random House of Canada Limited, Toronto. Originally published in the German Democratic Republic as *Der fremde Freund* by Aufbau-Verlag, Berlin and Weimar, in 1982. Copyright © 1982 by Aufbau-Verlag, Berlin and Weimar. First English translation published in hardcover by Pantheon Books, a division of Random House, Inc., in 1989.

Library of Congress Cataloging-in-Publication Data

Hein, Christoph, 1944–
The distant lover.
Translation of: Der fremde Freund.
I. Title.
PT2668.E3747F7413   1989   833'.914   88-42617
ISBN 0-679-72898-8

This translation has been made possible in part through a contribution from the Wheatland Foundation.

Manufactured in the United States of America

First American Paperback Edition

THE DISTANT LOVER

In the beginning was a landscape.

A background, cypress-green, a narrow line of gleaming crystalline emptiness. Then a bridge spanning an abyss, a gorge, a stream flowing far below. As we approach—not walking or striding, more like a camera zooming in—we realize the bridge is broken down, a ruin. Two beams spanning a bottomless deep. I, or this person who may be me, hesitate. I—let's say it is me—look around. My companion (his face remains dream-blurred, a man, definitely someone I know, a friend) raises his hands. We have to cross. There's no turning back. We must get to the other side. Far below, boulders, brambles, and water, dimly sensed. We step onto the bridge. A shiver runs through me. For the first three or four steps we cling to the railing. Then it ends, splintered, jagged, thrusting into the air, a severed torso. My companion places one foot on the beam and offers me his hand. He edges forward, standing sideways, sliding one foot out a few inches, then pulling the other one after it. I slip off my shoes, take his hand, my left foot tests the ground, the beam. His hand is clammy. He should let go of me, I think. Each for himself. But his fingers are digging into my hand and won't let go. I keep my eyes fixed on the line of trees opposite, so as not to look down. Down into the abyss. I know if I look, I will fall. We've only started, and the beam seems to stretch on interminably. Slowly we edge forward. An unexpected change in the cypress-green background, a movement along our side of the chasm. At first an indistinguishable flickering in the air, then, all too distinct against the glistening void, five runners emerge from the woods, one after the other. Their shorts are white, and a rune-like symbol adorns their jerseys. I want to point them out to my companion. I speak, I shout, but cannot hear a sound. I cannot hear my own voice. The runners are nearing the bridge. Our bridge. They run evenly, with the elegant, regular movement of machines. Muscular young men with open, glowing faces, panting but not straining. With amazement I notice how alike they are—they could be brothers. Quintuplets running toward the shattered bridge. I shout at them to stop. My mouth moves without a sound. All remains silent. It frightens me that I can make out their faces. Not like my companion's cloud-face. Each feature stands out clearly: sculpted, sharp, masculine. They've reached the bridge. They keep their pace steady. They rush toward us on the second beam, past us, heading for the other bank. I see their even movements, their panting mouths, yet still there is no sound. A silent scene. My companion is gripping me tightly. His nails are cutting into my arm. We stand, transfixed. The other beam trembles after the runners have crossed, and then grows still. We could go on. Or maybe we should turn back. But for us there is no turning back; we have to cross. And now it is even more hopeless.

Then the images vanish. Fog, or grayness, or nothingness.

And now, the sound. The measured footsteps of the runners evenly hammering, like clockwork. The quivering beam, the soft whistle of an amplitude. Finally a high tone, echoing away. Imageless. Asynchronic.

Later, much later, attempts at reconstruction. Re-creation of an event. Hoped-for approximation. To grasp, to comprehend. Its precise nature remains uncertain. A dream. Or a distant remembering. An image I cannot reach, nor ultimately understand. Nonetheless a reassuring presence within the nameless, inexplicable entity that is also me. Finally the desire passes. Finished. Buried beneath my over-real reality, beneath images of my daily life, gaudy, loud, insignificant. Healing. And only the terror, the experience of utter helplessness, remains inside me, elusive, ineradicable.

1

· ·

Even on the morning of the funeral I still wasn't sure whether
I'd go. And since I didn't know what I would decide by
noon, I took my mid-season coat out of the closet. It was
a dark blue that might pass for black, with a rabbit-fur
collar. It was obviously wrong for warm weather, but I
didn't want to run around all day in a black suit. And in

case I did decide to go, it seemed just as inappropriate to
turn up at the cemetery in a summer dress. The coat was
a compromise. In case I actually went. I draped it over my
arm before locking the door to my apartment.

I had to wait for the elevator. The officer from Frau
Rupprecht's apartment was standing between the two elevator doors, pressing both call buttons. He too had a coat
over his arm, a sort of military raincape. Maybe he was with
the police and not the army. I can't tell all their uniforms
apart. A bag stuck out from under his cape, some kind of
attaché case. He nodded to me when I approached, then
without a word turned back to the elevator buttons. He
kept tapping out a rhythm with the toe of his boot.

Somewhere in the depths of the elevator shaft came a
rustling, a vibration of steel cables, the promise of a change
long wished for, the sort of hope that fosters patience. Then
the light appeared behind the little window. The officer
slid the door open and got into the elevator, which wasn't
empty. With my bulky coat over my arm, I pushed in
behind him. The stolid faces became downright unfriendly.
A silent descent into the depths. The elevator stopped twice,
but no one got out, no one got in. I stared wordlessly at
the faces pressing in all around me, and was stared at in
turn, just as wordlessly and directly. An undesired intro-
duction with all our senses, especially offensive to the sense
of smell.

Down in the lobby I glanced at the mailboxes. Nothing
but newspapers; the mail would come later. The death notice
was still posted. A standard form, with name, cemetery,
and time of day written in blue ball-point. Someone had
tacked it to the bulletin board. Probably the building superintendent. He must have got it in the mail. Eventually

he'll get notices like that for everyone in the building who dies. And that, aside from fixing a leaky faucet, or taking a screwdriver to an accidentally locked door which he then opens with a powerful shove of his shoulder, will be the only personal contact he has with the tenants.

I doubt this notice means anything to anyone. Too many people die in my building. There are simply too many old people here. Every month these sheets of paper bordered in black hang on the bulletin board for three or four days, until someone pulls them down. I doubt if anyone in the building besides me knew Henry. He would have mentioned it.

I laid my coat on the back seat and drove to the hospital.

There was a note under my door. The chief was asking me to go with him to the mayor's office that afternoon. He had requested an appointment because the housing commission had taken two rooms away from the hospital. Our space allotment had never been reduced before. We need those rooms so we can recruit nurses from the provinces; they won't work for us unless we can give them a room in Berlin. I had no idea why he wanted me to come along. Maybe he thought I was still the social-welfare steward for the union. I'd given up that position last year. Or maybe he just wanted company. Our chief of staff was known for liking to appear with a retinue wherever he went. I was to call him right away.

At eight-fifteen the nurse, Carla, arrived. As always she rushed into my office, saying she was a bit late because of the children—you know. Carla's a bit late every day, and it always has something to do with the children. I'm sure she only mentions it because she thinks I'll feel guilty. She's the type of woman who clings to her domestic role. That cow-eyed, steamy bliss is something we won't let go; after all, it's our purpose in life. We live for our children, who live for their children, who live . . . Apparently humankind has fallen into a vicious circle. The succession of generations—all based on false premises. The devil as past master of the syllogism. That might make for a nice rude awakening someday. But for the time being, life does have a meaning. At least Carla thinks so. She's also sure she knows what caused my divorce. She's convinced my husband left me because I failed to present him with chubby little babies, or because I don't have a large bust, or because I don't use makeup.

When Carla opened the wardrobe and saw my coat, she asked if I was going to a funeral. I was annoyed I hadn't left it in the car. Her asking decided the matter: I would go to the cemetery that afternoon. Any reservations I might have felt vanished in the face of her tactlessness. I could feel myself tensing with anger. Then came the usual remarks—a relative? Oh, a friend, how awful, was he young? Oh, that's really terrible, I know how you must feel, you look so pale. I busied myself with some files. Carla was changing into her uniform. Since the file cabinet and storage cupboards were in the front room, they had put our wardrobe into my office. So my nurse had to come in here to change, wash up, and do her hair. Carla's very big on grooming. She contrives to hop around in her brassiere for hours, busy with her nails or applying various lotions. One time she told me she felt all sweaty, an expression that nauseated me.

While Carla was changing, I phoned the chief. I said I had to go to a funeral that afternoon. He didn't comment. I was relieved he didn't try to express his sympathy. I also told him that the new woman in ophthalmology had taken over my position in the union. She hadn't been around long enough to come up with any plausible excuse for not serving. I pointed out to him that she was prettier and younger than I. He pretended to be indignant and talked about my charm, which had supposedly made him my eternal captive. Then he hung up. Carla went out into the front room. I could hear her unlock the door and call in the patients.

Just before lunch Herr Doyé came to see me. He's seventy-two, of French Huguenot descent. Married to a woman who's paralyzed, which doesn't prevent him from regularly "doing it" with her, as he puts it. He loves to talk about his sex life. Which probably explains why he comes in every week. There's nothing wrong with him. He sits in my office for five minutes, tells me what a man he used to be and still is. Then I throw him out, and he goes to sit with Carla or with the other patients in the waiting room, where he continues in the same vein. Last week he brought me a lipstick. He insisted that I try it right away. When I twisted the bottom part, up came a little dark-red phallus made of plastic. He thought it was hilarious. He said the two of us knew what the score was, there wasn't a thing anyone could tell us. He's a dirty, disgusting, very nice old man. Some days I find him quite bearable and hear him out. Sometimes I can't stand him and send him on his way immediately.

Today all he talked about was the funeral I was going to. That birdbrain Carla had told him about it. Now he wanted to hear how well I'd known Henry, and whether I'd "done it" with him. Finally he went out to sit with Carla. She often complains about his pawing her, but I'm not sure she really minds. I suspect she's one of those women who will let a man do anything he wants just because he's a man. In any case, I have no intention of giving old Doyé a talking-to, as Carla says I should. She's a grown woman who can take care of herself. Why should I hurt a poor old man's feelings, when all he wants is to kill time until his television program comes on?

At lunch I noticed that the chief had already invited the new doctor to sit at his table. He winked at me and motioned toward her with his head. I sat down at my usual place and started in on my vegetable soup. My colleagues had heard about the funeral and asked a few questions out of politeness. But in fact no one cared, and soon we were back to the usual topics. One of the doctors from radiology had had his car stolen three weeks ago. He had bought it only a few months before that, for twice the book value. The police told him there was no hope of finding it, and referred him to the insurance company. Which, it turned out, would cover only a fraction of the book value. For three weeks he's talked about nothing else, and most of the others share his outrage. I think he'd kill the thief if he could catch him. The Hippocratic Oath has its limits. Like everything else.

After lunch I went out for a cup of coffee with Anne. Anne's three years older than I am. She started out as a dentist but had to give it up a few years ago, because her wrists tend to get inflamed. She went back to medical school and became an anesthesiologist. She has four children and a husband who rapes her every two weeks or so. Apart from that they enjoy their sex life, which is pretty regular, she says, but now and then he rapes her. She says he needs it. She doesn't want a divorce because of the children and because she's afraid of being alone. So she puts up with it. Whenever she's had a drink or two she starts to bitch and moan about her husband. But she stays with him. I keep my distance. It's a strain being friends with a woman who's resigned to her own degradation. Her husband, who's also a doctor, is fourteen years older. Now she's just waiting for him to "go limp." Senility as hope. I suppose there are crazier things to look forward to.

At the café Anne is quite the lady: the doctor having her coffee. The usual flirtation with the proprietor. She'd probably flinch if he put his hand on her shoulder. She shows off her new suit, black with a lilac scarf. Her husband bought it for her yesterday. She says it was terribly expensive, but he paid for it without a word. The present after. Poor Anne. Maybe I should borrow the suit. It would be more appropriate for the cemetery than my heavy coat. On the other hand, what do I want with her rapes? God knows she's earned the right not to have to share her suit with anyone.

She talked about a poetry reading she'd heard in a church last week. People had asked the poet all sorts of political questions, and he sidestepped them diplomatically, with a nice sense of humor. I tried not to stare at her plate. She was already on her third piece of cake. I knew that if I so much as mentioned it, her eyes would immediately fill with tears, so I kept quiet. There's no way to help her. Let her eat cake; her figure can stand it.

We ordered one more brandy. Then I said good-bye. I stopped at the office to get my dark coat. Carla was on the phone with a patient and waved frantically for me to wait. I made signs I was in a hurry and slipped out.

Around lunchtime the streets are empty, so I could drive fast. I stopped at a flower shop on the way and bought nine white carnations. The closer I got to the cemetery, the more nervous I felt. It occurred to me that I hadn't thought about

Henry all day. Even now all I could think of was that I was supposed to remember him. It wasn't too late to turn around, go home, grab my camera, and spend the afternoon driving around taking pictures. Henry certainly didn't expect me to "pay my last respects." To him, funerals and sickbed visits were like other people's marital quarrels you overhear without meaning to. They're unpleasant and turn you into a voyeur. A waste of time. Atavistic cults of the dead. Toying, though not admitting it, with the hope of eternity, never quite abandoned. Or else plain gloating: Look who's burying whom! After all, there are funeral homes that handle these things professionally, impeccably. Why be there in person? Solidarity with a corpse? Why do people feel compelled to actually be there when they throw the dirt on someone or slide him into the oven? Why do they feel they must? It isn't the person you loved any longer. I had hoped Henry would be buried in Dresden. Dresden is far enough away that it would have been easy to decide not to go.

The engine began to knock. I shifted into neutral and pumped the accelerator twice. Remember to get gas afterward, I told myself.

I parked on a side street, even though there were plenty of spaces in front of the cemetery. I sat in the car for a few seconds, my mind quite blank. Then I took the flowers, got out, and wrapped the coat over my shoulders.

From the cemetery gate I could see people standing outside the chapel, waiting in two groups. Probably the undertaker was late, and each group was waiting to be called in and processed. It struck me that I had never met any of Henry's relatives. Which group was I supposed to join? Given my distaste for funerals, it would be ironic if I ended up at a total stranger's. But I didn't know whom to ask. I didn't even know how to phrase the question. Excuse me, which corpse do you belong to?

I had hoped to see Henry's colleague, a familiar face as a token of my right to be there. He was not in either group. I had stopped short, and everyone turned to stare at me. The awkward waiting for solemnity, the self-conscious, muted comments about the departed, about the future, about fate, about the likelihood of rain. The conversational possibilities are limited, and all talk breaks off with the arrival of someone new. A liberating apparition: now it's all right to examine the stranger in silence.

I pulled a pack of cigarettes out of my handbag, but put them back immediately. Ashes to ashes, but smoking isn't very acceptable.

They were still staring at me. Obviously we were all troubled by the same question: to whom do I belong, to which corpse? Was there someone I was supposed to say hello to? I entered the flower shop just inside the gate. As I opened the door, a bell tinkled. Inside, a wet, tiled rotunda, green plants and white bows. A bead curtain separated the shop from the workroom behind. Through the window I could see the groups waiting in front of the chapel. The saleswoman came out, a gaunt woman in black with deep creases around her mouth. It comes with the business, the proximity to death.

May I help you?

She looked at my carnations.

Could you tell me which funeral is taking place now?

Ask the sexton.

Her voice was weary. Now she was convinced of what she had already suspected: I wasn't buying anything.

Where would I find the sexton?

Somewhere around there.

She pointed in the direction of the cemetery. Then she went toward the back room and stood there surrounded by the bead curtain, watching until I left the shop.

Outside I looked at the window display and wondered what to do. Maybe I was at the wrong cemetery altogether, maybe Henry was being buried somewhere else while I stood waiting here. In the glass I could see the door to the chapel opening. I turned around. A man came out, small, his head bowed. He said something, but I couldn't make it out. One group began to move, and then stopped a few steps outside of the chapel. I went over to them. Just as I was about to speak to the little man, he asked me if I was part of the "Henry Sommer service." I nodded. He said it would be starting in a few minutes.

I was standing in the middle of about twenty people, who now examined me even more boldly. I straightened my coat and stared alternately at my flowers and the toes of my shoes.

When the doors to the chapel swung open, we had to step aside. Four men carried out a coffin, and behind it walked three young men, with long, unkempt hair, none older than twenty. One of the young men noticed me watching. He raised his head, looked me in the eye for a moment, and grinned. I turned away. The double doors closed, then immediately opened again. The difficult rites of death. The little man with the stoop waved us inside. I followed the others. In front of the altar stood the coffin. The stooped man removed the wreaths and flowers and placed them around the platform. An arrangement: he deliberated, selected. The wreaths in the center, two inscribed bows carefully smoothed out. My carnations disappeared somewhere. In the first pew sat a woman with two children. She was in her mid-thirties. I noticed she was looking at me and I quickly moved to one of the pews in the rear. A soft crackle came over the loudspeaker, then the rustle of a needle on a record groove, a regularly recurrent surge and ebb, a whirring in the air. Then organ music: a fugue, very loud. The little man, probably the sexton, lowered the volume slightly. He was sitting on a chair up front, next to the record player. A small door on the same level as the altar opened, and a minister appeared. He went to a lectern, placed a book on it, and then seemed to be absorbed in prayer. After a while he raised his head and looked over to the sexton. Finally he coughed discreetly. The sexton looked up, carefully turned the volume very low, and lifted the needle off the record. A soft crackling marked the end of the music. Next the minister spoke. He talked about Henry. For a moment I had the silly thought that he was reading from Henry's résumé because he intended to hire him. The words he spoke were mellifluous, well chosen, kindly, and he had a beautiful voice. He addressed the widow, the young woman with the two children in the first row. I wondered whether she noticed the minister's gentle voice. It really was strikingly pleasant. It exuded confidence and self-satisfaction. He was undoubtedly vain. Would a minister also cheat on his wife? I leafed through the hymnal that had been lying on my seat. Prescribed songs, prescribed gestures. The proper conduct for every occasion. The advantages of an ancient tradition. No problems about what to wear. When I perforce shall part this world, do not Thou part from me. Death as homecoming. I had no idea Henry was a believer. He probably had no idea either. Survivors revise the story. If my corpse should fall into the hands of an Indian sect, presumably I would be transformed into dust Hindu-style. The sexton put the needle back on the record. A pity—I would have liked to go on listening to the minister. He speaks well, my grandmother would say when she found a man attractive. He speaks well, this minister. She would certainly have liked him.

Henry's wife sat with her head bowed. Now and then she whispered something to the children. Admonitions, probably. I could see only her back.

The music came to an end, the sexton turned off the record player. Then he slipped over to the little door the minister had used before. He opened it and beckoned. The four men wearing grease-spotted top hats, who had already carried the first coffin out of the chapel, appeared and took up their positions. The little man with the stoop quickly removed the wreaths and bouquets. And while the minister, his book tucked under his left arm, went up to Henry's widow, shook her hand, and whispered a few words, the men raised the coffin with practiced movements and placed it on their shoulders. They took three steps; then the sexton stopped them. A kind of master of mourning ceremonies. The minister fell in behind the coffin with the woman and the children. Now the other guests rose, took their wreaths and flowers, and formed a line. A procession. Since I was sitting in the last pew, everyone else was standing, ready to march, when I finally got hold of my carnations. They looked wilted against the black cloth. The sexton opened the double doors and gave the pallbearers a sign.

The way to the grave seemed endless. The pallbearers wove in and out among the gravestones. I felt hot but didn't want to take off my coat now. Then I saw the freshly dug grave. The men placed the coffin on wooden planks that had been laid across the hole. They then unrolled canvas straps, passed them under the coffin, and draped them over their shoulders. One of the men removed the boards, holding the coffin by a strap. Slowly the pallbearers lowered it into the ground. I was standing where I could watch the woman. She was constantly talking at the pale children. The minister guided her to an iron bowl filled with earth. He took a handful and threw it on the coffin. Then she stepped up to the grave, and then the children. They took their places by the open excavation. Everyone who threw earth approached them afterward, pressed their hands, or embraced them.

I was astonished at how little noise the earth made falling on the wooden coffin. It was a soft rustling, and I had expected a thump. Clods of earth thumping down on the coffin lid. I'd read that somewhere. My hand was dirty. It seemed improper to clap my hands. So I just rubbed my fingers together gently, which didn't do much good. I could feel the earth when I shook hands with Henry's wife. We looked at one another. Her eyes were motionless, her gaze full of sorrow and hatred, as if she wanted to register my face once and for all. A homely, embittered woman, incessantly examining her life to find someone to blame for so much banality, so many faded hopes. She's going to hit you, she's going to slap you right here beside her husband's open grave, I said to myself. The thought amused me. I quickly pulled my hand away and hurried past the children. The minister then offered me his hand. I waited for him to say something, some meaningless sentence in his soft voice. But he only squeezed my hand and radiated his practiced sympathy. Too bad, pastor. A few steps from the grave, the funeral party regrouped. They were waiting for the end of the ceremony, for the wife, the children. I walked past them quickly, just hoping I wouldn't get lost. I thought I could feel the wife's eyes on my back. After a bend in the path, I finally took off my coat and folded it over my arm. As I did, I turned around. All I saw were gravestones and motionless, dusty trees.

For a while I drove through the city aimlessly. Later I drank some brandy in a café near my apartment, trying to remember Henry. An act of piety that I thought I owed him. Two men came up to my table and sat down. They were a little drunk and wanted to talk. One of them had a dark-red birthmark on his right cheek. They ordered schnapps for themselves and for me. I refused. I wanted to think of Henry, of Henry who was dead, of the funeral, of the soft, sexy voice of the minister. Then I gave up.

2

· ·

I knew Henry for a year. His apartment in our high-rise
was on the same floor as mine. The building consists of one-
room apartments. Nowadays they call them studios. When
I was a child I pictured something entirely different when
I heard the word studio. They were frequently found in
novels, where they were populated by artists in velvet jackets

and berets, ladies in flowing gowns and gentlemen in evening dress. Rooms in which all the senses received constant intense stimulation. Our studios are different. Their only inhabitants are lonely souls, old folks, unmarried people like me. In the summer a bad odor comes from the garbage chute and sometimes from the toilets. All day long, radio music drones through the building. Even on Sunday mornings. The whole place is full of all kinds of noises. They pass through the walls along the pipes. A muffled babble of voices that never dies down. You get used to it, you stop hearing it. The only time it's quiet here is late at night. Even then, the radiators send their clanks up and down the building.

I don't know when Henry moved in. The tenants in this building change so often. The young ones get married, the old ones die. People live here subject to recall on short notice. In transit. It's not worth getting to know anyone. I don't much care for that anyway—acquaintances who live in the same building. You run into them every day, you can't avoid conversations. Mandatory friendliness is a burden. When you're divorced, the need to steer clear of those unavoidable, unchanging daily civilities seems to grow even stronger. I no longer have any desire to stare into the faces of strangers who are supposed to be part of my life just because they're there, day in, day out. Inescapable familiarity, and I'm at its mercy. I prefer the more neutral relationship I have with the pieces of furniture in my apartment. They aren't so demanding. Their presence has a certain dignified charm. But I don't really care about that either.

Back in April, or maybe it was May, I was standing by the elevator. In this building you're always waiting for the elevator. Maybe because the old people press the wrong buttons so often. Or maybe two elevators just aren't enough for a building that has twenty stories and so many tenants.

I saw Frau Rupprecht, my neighbor, appear at the end of the corridor. The old woman took a few steps in my direction, her head trembling. Then she stopped and put her hand to her temple. Her eyes blinked helplessly, sunk in deep, creased hollows. I spoke to her, asked whether I could help her. She glanced at me but didn't really see me. Her hand stroked her temple as though she wanted to still some panicky terror, some inexpressible fear. But she calmed down, smiled, and greeted me, only to hurry back along the corridor and disappear into her apartment.

Then Frau Luban came out; she has the apartment next to the garbage chute. I was still waiting for the elevator. Frau Luban has trouble walking, but she spends the whole day hobbling through the building. On every floor she has acquaintances to sit and drink coffee with.

She stopped next to me and began complaining about the building superintendent, that he didn't do a thing. Besides which, he was insolent and talked back. Then she asked why I never came to see her. She knows I'm a doctor. Everybody on the floor knows I'm a doctor, and they all expect me to make house calls. They even come to me for pills.

I told her I was very busy, and she said she was sorry to hear that. She was calling me "dear child" now, which puzzled me. Then she said she had something to tell me in confidence. I stared at the little window and hoped the elevator would come. She said she was a member of the tenants' committee and that the police had come to see them. A gentleman in uniform had asked them to keep an eye out. They should report anything suspicious—unusual visitors, frequent parties, anything out of the ordinary. Frau Luban's eyes swam behind her thick glasses. The police know what they're doing, she said. She paused for a moment, waiting for me to say something. I could hear the elevator move and then stop somewhere in the building. I pressed the call button several times and wondered whether I should take the stairs.

The old lady sidled up close to me and asked whether I hadn't noticed anything about the tenant in apartment 7. He was a strange one. I shook my head and said I didn't spy on people.

That's not what this is, she replied in a huff. She was standing so close I could smell her cheap pink powder. A mixture of primness and poverty. And I pictured myself thirty years from now, with powdered cheeks, scurrying through the corridors of this building, eagerly sucking in the sounds from other people's apartments and celebrating every night I survived as a victory.

Frau Luban touched my arm. She kept her head bowed and whispered: Look over there.

I turned around. A man in a felt hat was coming along the corridor. That's him, Frau Luban hissed, and turned away.

The man pushed the glass door open with his foot and joined us in front of the elevator. He observed me intently. I stared back at him, just as silently. His face was irregular, as if it were put together out of two different halves. The felt hat looked ridiculous. Or maybe just the cocky way he wore it.

The elevator arrived, and we got in. I stayed by the door. The old lady pressed up close to me, which made me uncomfortable. I moved my bag between us. The man was standing behind me. Suddenly there was a yowl, a brief, whining cry, as though someone had kicked a dog. Frau Luban grabbed my arm tightly. I shook her off and turned around. The man in the felt hat was leaning against the back wall, looking up at the illuminated numbers in obvious boredom. We smiled at each other. When we reached the lobby, he gave me a friendly hello and held the door for me.

That evening Henry came to my apartment. I was already in bed when the doorbell rang. I put on a bathrobe and opened the door. He was standing there with a smoking, evil-smelling pot in his hand and asked whether I could help him. I replied that it was late and I'd already gone to bed. He said he hadn't had anything to eat, and this—he raised the pot—was inedible. Then he brushed past me into the room. He sat down in my easy chair and looked at the photographs on the walls. I stood by the door and told him I was tired, I had to get some sleep. He said he wouldn't stay long, he just wanted something to eat, then he would go. I went into the kitchen. He stayed in the chair and continued to talk.

Later he sat down at the table and ate. He wanted me to sit with him. I said I really had to get some sleep. Did I take the photographs? he asked. Did I develop them myself? It felt good to have him there. I was pleasantly weary and crawled back into bed. I lay there with my eyes closed and listened to him. He was still talking about my photographs and the landscapes they depicted. Then he talked about the room, saying that everybody in the building had set up their apartments the same way. The smallness of the room and the uniform floor plan forced everyone to put the bed here, the table there. Only one variation was possible, and it too left no choice: if you owned books and needed shelves, the bookcase had to go next to the door, and then the only space for the bed was by the window. And when he thought about the very same books occupying the very same places on all those shelves, it made him want to put a bullet through his head, he said cheerfully. I listened to his voice and felt pleasantly sleepy. He got up and paced back and forth. He stared out the window and then went back to the table to get something to drink. I lay in bed and watched him. Then he caught sight of my high-heeled gold sandals in a corner of the room. He was much taken with them and wanted me to put them on right away.

I said, You've eaten, now go. I need my sleep.

He didn't respond. He stood there with my sandals in his hands and admired them. Then he sat down in the easy chair, lit a cigarette, and stared out the window. He asked me whether I liked to go out on the balcony. He said he couldn't stand it himself.

Are you afraid of heights? I asked.

He shook his head. No, he said, It's something else.

Then he talked about me and about the possibilities and impossibilities of understanding another person. He asked me questions I couldn't answer. Meanwhile he smiled and drank red wine. I didn't understand him. I didn't know whether his talk, his weighty questions, were serious or teasing. Maybe it was all just a game, a sort of test. Certainly he seemed relaxed and chipper.

So what about the balcony? I reminded him. And what does it have to do with all this?

I'm just afraid of flying away, he said happily. Or, to be more prosaic, of falling. Something's got to happen: I'm alive, but what for? This incredible joke, the fact that I'm here in the world must have some point. So I keep waiting to find out.

He amused me.

Experience shows, I said, that this particular joke usually has a simple, ordinary punch line. And no matter how special you think it's going to be for you, it won't be all that different.

Yes, yes, he said, experience. And yet, experience sometimes presents us with a pair of gold sandals.

And that's enough for you?

It's enough for this evening, he replied softly. Then he asked, Are you still tired?

I shook my head. I didn't know what to think of him. And I had no desire to puzzle over it. He sat in the chair and smoked. Then he put out his cigarette and got into bed with me. I was too astonished to say anything.

He slept restlessly and got up early. I wanted to make breakfast for him, but he said I should stay in bed. Then he kissed me delicately and left. I went back to sleep. When I woke again, I stayed in bed trying to figure out what time it was. I thought of Frau Luban and the way she kept her door cracked, keeping watch over the whole corridor.

I got up, took a long shower, and put water on for coffee. Then I took the elevator down to check the mail. Only the newspaper was in the box. When I got back upstairs, the kitchen was full of steam. I made a pot of coffee and had breakfast, talking to myself as I did. It used to bother me when I caught myself talking out loud, but it doesn't anymore. It's even sort of comforting: there's music on the radio, and a human voice can be heard. What's the difference if it's my own?

Thinking about Henry, I went to the balcony door and opened it. I looked down into the street, then returned to the table and my breakfast. I had the newspaper open by my cup and read the classified section.

I never read anything but the classifieds. Publicly sanctioned and welcomed revelations. Restrained exhibitionism. Coded data on individual fates, ending discreetly with box numbers. The lost dog who answers to the name Trixie and never bites; the new bedroom set for sale, still under the original warranty; the ideal companions who offer themselves, or are themselves being sought, with interchangeable descriptions: interested in good books, the theater, travel; serious, responsible, conscientious, good sense of humor, nonsmoker. Or officially formulated grief: incomprehensible, inexpressible, shaken, a tragic loss. The conventional flourishes of these ads, life support for the inarticulate misery of the linguistically impaired. Occasionally at the hospital I get a glimpse of the background. Some nearby hospital provided a bed, an operating room, a death certificate. My colleagues know the whole story and are eager to share it.

Then there's the game of buy and sell, speculators in collectibles, con men, swindlers, hopes for material happiness, or else desperate circumstances, raw need. A compendium of the city, a social novel with all the traditional elements. Including the perennial message about the march of generations.

Suddenly I heard a woman's voice in my apartment, calling someone. I had left the door to the balcony open, and Frau Rupprecht was standing on the next balcony scattering bird feed. The old woman had put on a black woolen stole. Her hand was stretched out over the railing, her head wobbled slowly from side to side. She kept on with her little summoning cries, but birds don't visit our building. The wind blows the crumbs away. Frau Rupprecht rings my bell now and then to ask for some medication or other. Aside from that, she doesn't force herself on me.

I cleared the table and washed the dishes. Then I sat down and smoked a cigarette. There was nothing to tidy up. In such a small apartment there's very little to do.

Half an hour later I went to work.

3

. . . .

For the next three days I didn't see Henry. I was on call at
night, which meant that I didn't get to change clothes for
thirty-two hours. My shift was pretty quiet. In the emergency room the usual cases: intoxication, appendicitis,
stomach cramps, high blood pressure. On the wards intra-

venous meds, elevated blood-sugar levels, two transfusions, one case of respiratory distress. Around midnight some of the other doctors came over to have a cup of coffee with me. Then the police brought in some people for blood tests. It was my turn to deal with the alcoholics, and I had to fill out two committal forms for the police. Later several more patients came in: a woman in her first pregnancy who thought something was going wrong; a case of intestinal colic; a woman with heart palpitations who was accompanied by her agitated, oldish husband.

Toward six in the morning the hospital became noisy again. Then I had time for a good breakfast with the other doctors and nurses from the night shift before my office hours began at eight.

I don't mind office hours after I've been on call: I take everything in as if through a woolen curtain. Sounds hardly penetrate; they're muted, they float to the floor. I'm in a mild mood and placid toward everyone. The patients seem very understanding; maybe Carla's told them I was up all night. The only time I mind it is during my period; then the pain in my back is worse.

On Friday I saw Henry again, in the lobby by the mailboxes. I was coming back from the hairdresser's and looked terrible. If he hadn't caught sight of me, I would have hurried past and gone upstairs to comb out my hair. He took my hand and kissed it. Then he said he'd waited for me, that he was glad to see me. We went upstairs. Outside my door we made a date for that evening, to go out to eat.

Two hours later he rang the bell. We took his car. He drove well but very fast, and I said so. Did it make me nervous? he asked. Should he slow down? I told him it didn't bother me, he'd be the one to get the ticket, after all. He laughed and speeded up. I had to hold onto the handgrip, which he found amusing.

We drove through the city to a little restaurant. The owner was named Richard. He shook Henry's hand when we came in and showed us to a table behind a small potted palm. Richard was in his mid-forties, stocky, with a generous belly that spilled over his belt, and slack, puffy cheeks. Henry and he had known each other a long time. He stood by our table and talked about his wife. Then he told us about a murder in the neighborhood; one of his waiters had been involved as a witness. Finally he recommended a combination of dishes, which Henry agreed to at once. After Richard left, Henry explained that he hadn't consulted me because Richard could be trusted, and might have been offended had I objected.

The food was good, which I told Richard when he came over to ask how we liked it. He told Henry that his car was giving him trouble, what should he do? Henry promised to stop by in a few days and take a look. Later I asked Henry whether his work had something to do with cars. He shook his head. He was an architect, he said, and spent most of his time building small, standardized, superfluous nuclear power plants, with the river sometimes on the right, sometimes on the left. And these projects were the exciting part of his job; the rest was really boring. Working with cars was something he did for fun, a hobby.

We drank quite a bit of wine, and I talked a lot, as I always do when I drink. I think I also behaved rather aggressively; I found Henry's ironic self-possession annoying, and I tried to get a rise out of him. For some reason I wanted to make him really angry. I no longer know why. I didn't succeed. Henry merely smiled.

When coffee was served, Richard came and sat down with us. He talked about the murder again and about his waiter. Then on and on about his car, which he just couldn't understand but needed desperately. Henry was embarrassed; he could tell I wasn't interested.

Shortly before midnight we got up to go. I asked Henry to leave his car there and call a taxi. He asked me again whether I was nervous. I got very angry and replied that I was not impressed and didn't find it especially clever to drive drunk. Nevertheless I got into his car.

During the drive I observed him. He had pushed his felt hat to the back of his head and was driving with great concentration. He held the steering wheel only with the tips of his fingers. He shifted often. His movements were smooth, almost tender. I thought he must enjoy driving a car very much. He noticed that I was watching him and smiled, a little bashfully.

I said I had the feeling the car meant a lot to him. He agreed.

A little while later he said, When I'm driving, I feel alive.

That's quite a statement, I remarked.

True, he admitted.

Isn't there anything else? I asked. Besides that?

Nothing as intense, he said.

I said I didn't share his passion for driving, I couldn't really understand it. He replied that he didn't expect me to. It was a totally private pleasure, just for him.

So it's like one of those secret, solitary vices? I asked.

He nodded. The comparison amused him.

Then I asked whether he had a dream profession. Without a moment's thought he answered: I'd like to be a race car driver or a stunt man. A stunt man for high-speed chases.

Wouldn't that be rather dangerous?

He smiled. Of course, and rather alive.

Aren't you afraid of accidents? I asked.

There are doctors, he said, and looked at me.

Yes, I said, but there are also fatal accidents.

He said nothing, just pulled his mouth down at the corners. After some time he said, I'm not afraid of dying. It's worse for me not to be alive. Not to really live.

I was feeling somewhat nauseated from the alcohol. I leaned back and closed my eyes.

You're crazy, my friend, I said. Then I fell asleep.

At home he kissed me, and I said I found him quite strange. He wanted to know why, but I didn't explain. I couldn't, I didn't understand it myself. Something about him was incomprehensible to me, I sensed that, and I knew that this distance between us would remain. But I was too drunk to think about it; later I often did. However, I never have the urge to analyze something that I like just as it is.

The distance between us gave our relationship a cool familiarity that I found pleasant. I had no desire to reveal myself completely to another person again. I enjoyed caressing another's skin without wanting to crawl inside it.

Perhaps my reserve was merely a sign of age. But the question didn't interest me. I was content the way I was, I didn't want to speculate about it.

The next morning we had breakfast together. During the meal he performed little magic tricks with the cutlery and his soft-boiled egg. He was in a good mood. I told him I was going to drive to the country for the weekend; I had to visit someone. He wanted to come along but I said it was impossible. He didn't ask why. Suddenly I didn't want to go, but I had promised my mother I'd come. It was too late to call and cancel. Still I put off leaving.

I started a game of chess with Henry, then broke it off because I felt myself getting edgy. Visits to my parents always make me edgy. Hours before, I'm already tense about these courtesy calls on people I have no real ties with. Maybe my bad temper simply comes from the fact that these two people have the right to call me daughter, to feel proud of my successes, give me advice, force me to accept a cake or a jar of homemade preserves when I leave. They insist on their rights and always feel hurt that I come so seldom. I'm sure they don't feel any connection with me either, but they won't admit it. They wouldn't allow themselves to entertain such a thought. The accidental bond continues to be asserted, some unidentifiable obligation, requiring senseless activity like these superfluous visits.

When Henry got up to go, I asked him what he had planned for the weekend. He stood in the doorway, looked at me, and thought about it. His felt hat was pushed to the back of his head.

Probably nothing special, he said. He leaned forward to give me a quick kiss and left.

That evening I was at my parents'. I arrived late (We were already thinking you had forgotten us, child), and they were sitting in front of the television. The table was still set for me, even the cake from the afternoon was still out (We waited so long, Aunt Gerda too; you must go by to see her, she's so fond of you, child). I was tired and irritable, but I pulled myself together. A slip of paper, a wish list of medications, lay on the sideboard. Mother gave me one every time I visited. I had to get the prescriptions filled and mail them to her, so she could distribute them all over the neighborhood. I owe it to people, she remarked; I don't want them to think you're stuck-up just because you're a doctor now.

At eleven I went to bed. Father stayed in front of the television. He wouldn't go to sleep until the bottle of schnapps was empty.

When I was lying there in my old bed, Mother came in. She sat down on the edge of the bed and said we had to talk, there were so many things we never talked about. I said I didn't understand what she meant. She looked sad and asked why I was so cold to her, so unloving. I protested mildly, but without conviction, simply to avoid a quarrel.

I felt sorry for the woman sitting next to me, but except for that I couldn't muster any feeling for her. I didn't understand why she was sad that we didn't have a more loving relationship. We saw each other seldom, so seldom that it couldn't really matter to her either. But she was full of self-pity and cried some, and that made me sorry. Then she said that Father wasn't doing well. At the factory they had forced him to retire although he wanted to go on working. There had been some incident—he slapped an apprentice—and the management gave him a choice between retiring immediately or giving up his position as foreman. Father quit the next day. And the ceremony for his sixty-fifth birthday was canceled on the grounds that an award would be inappropriate at the time. The management promised that he could have it in a year or two, but the whole affair hurt him deeply. He broke off all contact with the plant and the other workers. Since he had no friends, now he was just sitting around the house.

Mother said she was having a very hard time with him; as she said this, she stroked my hand. I didn't know how to respond. It seemed strange that she expected me to comfort her. This was something she'd have to get through on her own. Besides, if I touched her, she would just start crying again.

Then she told me she had run into Hinner. Hinner is my ex-husband. He had been very, very nice to her, had driven her into town and gone way out of his way to drop her off where she wanted. It sounded as though he would soon be made head physician. He hadn't remarried (He can't get you out of his mind, child). He asked all sorts of questions about me, and would like to see me again. Wouldn't I like to see him too? I told her it was pointless to dredge up the past. With his exalted new status he would certainly attract enough female attention at the hospital. Mother said Hinner was a very fine man. He regretted the stupid things he had done, I should give him another chance, not bear a grudge. I should think of myself too; after all, no one's getting any younger. I said I hadn't left him because of the other women, but because the whole thing had simply been a mistake. I added, maybe a little harshly, that she should stop trying to play the matchmaker.

Mother cried a bit more and then told me some things about the neighbors. As she was leaving, she asked if I didn't agree it was nice that we'd had a real talk. I didn't understand what she meant, but I said yes, it was nice.

Mother was relieved.

I lay awake for a long time, unable to sleep, and finally took two sleeping pills.

At breakfast Mother asked whether I still smoked so much, and Father wanted to know what I thought about China. I said I still smoked a lot and didn't know much about China. Father explained at length why China was such a burning issue for us. Then he asked whether I was following developments in Surinam, and exploded because I didn't know where Surinam was. He said I was an over-educated fool because I didn't read the paper. He had raised his children to take an interest in politics, and he was disappointed in me. I told him I had lots of problems at the moment that were more pressing than world affairs. And to calm him down, I said that when things got better with me I would read the paper again. That only made him madder. He pounded on the table, rattling the cups, and shouted at Mother when she tried to intervene. Then he went to his room.

Mother remarked that I shouldn't take it seriously, I knew how Father was. He made scenes like that with her too over politics.

Then I helped Mother in the kitchen, and after that we went to visit Aunt Gerda, who lives two streets over.

Aunt Gerda is Mother's sister, a fat, red-faced woman who speaks loudly and uninhibitedly, like her husband. When we came in they were both in the kitchen cooking a rabbit. We sat down in the living room. Uncle Paul brought some of his homemade currant liqueur, which was sweet and sticky.

They talked about me and my life in Berlin. Uncle Paul said he couldn't understand why no man had snapped me up yet, an attractive woman like me. He didn't know what was wrong with men nowadays. In his time they didn't let a good thing slip away. With that, he grabbed my breast.

Aunt Gerda shrieked and smacked his hand, and Mother was disgusted. Uncle Paul said they shouldn't carry on that way. After all, I had always been his favorite. Aunt Gerda gave him another glass of liqueur and shooed him into the kitchen to lard the rabbit.

Then Aunt Gerda showed me her bulging varicose veins and repeated what her doctor had said. She wanted to know what I thought, and I said her doctor was right. Mother and Aunt Gerda talked about a new department store that had just opened, and I went into the kitchen to help Uncle Paul.

I washed lettuce for salad, peeled potatoes, and watched him prepare the rabbit. The three middle fingers were missing from his right hand. He had lost them in the war, and I had always known him with a crippled hand. He braced the knife between the two remaining fingers and his palm and cut skillfully and quickly. Beads of sweat stood out on his nose, which was broad and splotched with red. Suddenly he washed his hands and went out. When he came back he showed me some airplane tickets from the travel agency. As a birthday surprise for my aunt, he was giving her a trip to the Black Sea. He had saved up for two years. I mustn't say a word; he planned to tell her only on the day of their departure, otherwise she would refuse to fly. She was afraid to. She'd never flown before, and she said an old dog couldn't learn how.

Uncle Paul laughed and said he'd be able to get this old dog moving again. His yellowish eyes almost disappeared in a thicket of wrinkles. His bald head, framed by tufts of thin gray hair, glowed pink. He was happy as a child about his secret, and whispered again that I mustn't say a word to my aunt or he wouldn't be able to hustle her onto the plane. Then he took the papers back to the bedroom, where he kept them hidden.

Mother came into the kitchen and said we had to go.

As we were leaving, Uncle Paul winked at me and made a gesture that caused Aunt Gerda to shriek, again half indignant, half amused. Mother didn't like his joking. She called him a disgusting old billy goat, and Uncle Paul pinched her on the cheek.

At home Father was sitting in front of the television, engrossed in a political round table. Mother scolded him for not getting anything ready. We both went into the kitchen. I made the salad while Mother prepared a roast. How did I manage, living alone? she asked. I said I enjoyed it, I had time for myself now. I could think about the things that were important to me, things that used to get lost in the daily shuffle. She understood, she said. Then she wanted to know whether I had a boyfriend, and I said no. After a pause she asked how I could stand that, as a woman. I laughed and told her that of course sometimes I slept with a man, if that's what she wanted to know. It wasn't so hard to arrange. Mother said she could easily believe it; I was young and pretty. But wasn't I sometimes scared of later, of getting old? It would be hard to live alone then. I told her I didn't worry about it.

We worked for some time in silence. I saw that she was thinking. She looked at me and said in a strange voice that maybe I was going about it the right way, better than she and the others had. But she'd been married so long now, and besides, I belonged to another generation. Then she hugged me. I was going about it the right way, she said again.

At lunch Father was embarrassed. He praised my salad

extravagantly and at such length that Mother got annoyed. I said I had to leave right after lunch, I wanted to be in Berlin before dark. Mother asked me to stay a while, we were getting along so well. And Father said he needed to go over the copies of the will he had made for my sister and me. I said I didn't want a copy, but Father insisted on having everything arranged. We agreed to discuss it on my next visit.

As we were saying good-bye, Father slipped a fifty-mark note into my pocket. I gave it back to him. I knew he was trying to apologize, but I didn't think it was necessary. He was interested in politics and I wasn't, or not very much. That's just the way it is. And if he found my attitude wrong, he still didn't have to apologize.

I told him I earned enough, he should buy Mother something nice instead. Then we all kissed each other and I got in my car.

As I was driving through Brandenburg I stopped twice, to photograph a tumble-down barn and the ruins of a two-story lumber mill with large, weathered signs that gave the owner's name, the hours of operation, and the kinds of lumber sold. Two people out for a walk watched me. One of them took down the number on my license plate, and I had to laugh. I wondered what he'd do with it.

It was late afternoon when I got back to Berlin. Henry wasn't home. I opened the door to my balcony. Then I took a long shower and washed my hair. I wanted to read, but I was too jumpy to concentrate. I looked on the shelf for a detective story that I might have half forgotten. There wasn't one, so I played solitaire and made myself some coffee.

In the evening I rang Henry's bell, but he still wasn't home. I fixed my supper and ate it in front of the television set. Some French domestic comedy was on. I didn't understand what was happening, maybe because I'd missed the beginning. In bed I thought about my parents, but with no real clarity. Just a vague kind of remembering. Soon I went to sleep.

4

. . . .

These days there are pots of green plants on many of the
balconies in my building. They look pale and dusty. I don't
have any myself. I'd like to grow flowers, maybe geraniums,
but that's impossible. The wind would tear the petals off.

The usual patients came to my office, the majority of

them just to pick up new prescriptions. The rest had minor infections, nothing significant.

As usual, my nurse provided a little excitement. Carla announced she'd stopped taking her birth control pills because she was putting on too much weight. As she spoke, she swiveled her hips in front of me to demonstrate. But she was really upset—afraid, she said, that she would "get knocked up" because her husband was "always at it."

I thought of a story one of the X-ray technicians told me. Last year on National Health Care Day there was a party at the hospital for all medical personnel. A speech, a few awards of money, and after that a lot to drink. At a late hour this technician came across Carla and the chief of staff in an office. They were "at it," and the technician locked them in. The chief had to call a guard to let them out. The other doctors were thrilled; no one ever suspected that the old man had his little flings too. (Everyone suspected it of Carla.) The surprise of it all added to their pleasure. A sense of relief: welcome, brother, to the temple of our shabby little deeds, to the bosom of these banal, pathetic intimacies.

My fat little Carla was something of a nymphomaniac, to tell the truth, and now she wanted me to believe she was trying to keep her husband off her?

She asked whether I could get her a copper IUD, a new contraceptive import from the West that had been much discussed lately. Without looking up I said she should ask the chief—he had better connections. She left my office without a word.

That afternoon I called a doctor I'd known at medical school who worked at the government hospital, gave her the necessary details, and asked her to find an IUD for

Carla. She couldn't promise anything but said I'd hear from her in a few days.

As we were leaving work, I told Carla I had made the call. She thanked me, but wasn't wildly grateful or even much surprised. She probably suspected why I'd done it. I depend on her; there aren't enough nurses at our hospital. She knew she didn't owe me anything. Even so, she said good-bye almost warmly. For a moment I had the feeling she wanted to shake my hand, but we stuck to the usual nods.

A horrible thought crossed my mind: If she had shaken my hand, from then on she would always have shaken it, once in the morning and once at the end of the day. A thoughtless act that becomes a habit, permanent, inescapable. As meaningless as it is deplorable, a ritual that acquires a life of its own. An established familiarity we could no longer end.

Sitting in the car I followed Carla with my eyes, amused at my hypersensitivity and yet glad I had avoided more intimacy.

Is it sensitivity? Or hysteria? A fear of being touched, an idiosyncrasy of mine. And why this need to label it? It was simple enough: I just didn't have any desire to touch her. I didn't want to, that's all. Why look for explanations, why drag in psychiatric terminology? A result of the scientific age: life as clinical diagnosis; speech, gestures, feelings, merely patterns of deviant behavior as defined by the categories of some abstract norm.

I turned the motor on. As I swung the car around, I saw Carla's back in the mirror. She was walking with a light swing, vigorously wiggling her behind. I felt sorry for her.

I didn't see Henry all week. Letters lay in his mailbox

untouched; I noticed them every day when I went down for the mail. Even so, I rang his bell and was disappointed not to find him. Only the door of the woman who lived next to him opened a crack, then closed loudly the minute I turned away. I didn't know where he was or why he hadn't told me he was going away. And I was surprised at myself for expecting him to. We weren't responsible for each other. Neither of us owed the other anything.

I tried not to think about him anymore. I was annoyed that I was so ready to surrender myself. Why should he tell me he was going away? Was I already throwing myself into a relationship again? A sort of marriage, with its thousands of little obligations and petty dependencies? Once should have been enough.

On Thursday I took my fur coat to the cleaner's after work. The woman at the counter asked whether I wanted to leave it for storage. It would be better for the fur to store it professionally. I asked her what that meant, but she couldn't tell me. She simply said many of their customers left their coats there for storage over the summer. I wanted to know whether they could also do small repairs, since a hook had come off the coat. She couldn't tell me that, either. She told me she had been divorced a year ago and was looking for a good job. She'd gone to the university for two years but had left to take care of her husband and children. Now it was hard for her to find an interesting job.

You see what it does to you?—love, I mean, she said. She hoped she could work as a potter, she'd always been creative. She used to do some weaving. If she had money, she'd open a little shop or an atelier for cloth and leather accessories.

She felt as if she could trust me, she said. She needed

someone she could talk to. Her husband had remarried, and she was living alone with her son and two daughters. The son was fifteen. He stole things from her, didn't come home nights, got drunk, and skipped school. She asked what my profession was, and I told her I was a doctor.

Almost frightened, she said, Oh excuse me, Doctor, please excuse me for going on like this.

The trust was gone. Now she talked only about my fur coat. It seemed to make her uncomfortable, discussing her personal problems with a doctor. That was fine with me; I couldn't help her anyway. I gave her a friendly good-bye and left my coat.

Then I bought a few groceries at the market and a white collarless blouse in a boutique. The little shop had no dressing room, and I hesitated to take the blouse without trying it on first. The saleswoman tried to persuade me. It would look terrific on me, she said. Then she commented on my figure; I was fantastically slim, she said, and the blouse only looked good on women with boyish figures like mine. I paid what she asked, though it seemed too much, because I wanted to get out of there quickly. The way she talked about my figure made me uncomfortable, and I was annoyed when she walked around me, looking me over, and commenting on my "bust."

As I was paying she kept on talking. She was larger than I, and her mouth was about level with my eyes. Her constantly moving lips pouted obsequiously, her hands fluttered at her breast, her scrawny neck was draped with chains. When she handed me my change, I looked around the tiny space and asked her where the bathroom was. She shook her head uncomprehendingly, and when I asked how she managed all day without a bathroom, she laughed nervously.

Her laughter seemed inappropriate to me, but since she didn't want to answer, I said: I understand. Then she blushed. Without a word she handed me the bag with the blouse and thanked me. I regretted having embarrassed her with my question. But suddenly the shop had seemed so confining that the question just popped out spontaneously, without any thinking on my part. The missing toilet as a technical problem. What I didn't know was that it was a human one as well. It wouldn't do any good to explain myself, I would only embarrass her more.

As I closed the door behind me and went down the steps to the sidewalk, I turned and looked into the tiny display window. For a moment our eyes met. She had her arms folded over her chest. Just for a moment, then they started fluttering again.

Behind me the air quivered with passing cars and the squeal of a streetcar. Then it grew quieter, until the next wave of vehicles came speeding up and streamed past me. Here and there lights had been turned on. The cloudy, impenetrable sky was now a uniform gray.

In the evening I went to the Kramers'. I've known Charlotte Kramer since medical school. Now she works at the university. Her husband Michael is the lab director at a pharmaceutical plant that tests medicines. He's ten years older than she and already bald. They're both well-balanced, nice people who live only for their children. I like them very much. They're uncomplicated. Evenings with them are tiring but soothing.

The lobby of their building had its usual somewhat sour smell. I breathed through my handkerchief as I went up the stairs. The door flung open when I rang the bell. The whole family—they have three boys—rushed forward to hug me. I handed out chocolate. Then I went into the children's room and was given a demonstration of a battery-operated car. The children were fighting, and I was relieved when Charlotte sent them off to take their baths. She gave me a tour of the apartment. At Charlotte's there's always something new to see. Her husband is handy, and he's forever building shelves or putting up paneling. This time I was expected to admire an adjustable storage rack mounted on the corridor ceiling. It looked dangerous. I praised his work, and he beamed at me. Like the papa in a French movie I saw once.

Later we had cheese fondue in the living room. Charlotte and Michael talked about the children, what they had done and the amazing things they'd said. They kept interrupting each other, enjoying it all. Then Michael showed some slides from a trip to Luxembourg. I drank a lot because I was bored. Charlotte got a little tipsy and made fun of Michael's baldness and his advanced age. Michael just laughed; he was used to her jokes.

In the kitchen Charlotte told me she was having an affair with a student who was taking correspondence courses at the university. He came to Berlin every six weeks, and they slept together in his furnished room. He was married too. She wanted to know whether she should tell Michael. I asked whether she wanted a divorce. She said no, she couldn't even say whether she loved the student. It was purely sexual, could I understand that? I said I could, and she said she couldn't, because Michael was so good. She felt bad and despised herself, but kept on sleeping with the student. Then she scalded her hand with the water she was boiling for coffee, and Michael came into the kitchen and sprayed Panthenol on her reddened skin.

After the coffee I said good-bye. Michael accompanied me downstairs to help me get a taxi. On the street he hugged me good-bye and tried to kiss me. I told him amicably that we shouldn't do that. He became embarrassed and wiped his glasses. I asked him to go back upstairs. I wanted to wait there alone until a taxi came by, but he stayed on, telling me about a conference in Basel, and the things he had brought back for Charlotte and the children.

When a taxi finally stopped, he tried to kiss me again. His glasses fell off, and I had to pick them up because he couldn't see to find them. He stood there with the eyes of a sorrowful puppy and waved to me.

5

. . . .

Early Saturday morning Henry rang my bell. He stood in
the doorway, his felt hat shoved back, and smiled at me
without saying anything. I asked him where he'd been, and
he said he wanted to sleep with me. He undressed me and
we made love all morning. In between I fixed breakfast,
and he told me he had been in Hungary for a week. He

and a group of colleagues had visited Hungarian cities to study how various technical installations had been rebuilt. A good trip but, on the whole, strenuous. His colleagues all drank a lot. They hit the cafés first thing in the morning, and since he wasn't a serious drinker, he had just been in their way. He described the Hungarian farmers' markets and the thermal baths. When I asked why he hadn't told me he was going away, he didn't reply. I lay beside him and waited for him to answer. I sensed that he was annoyed, but I didn't care.

I thought, he said finally, that we had an understanding. Then he lit a cigarette and looked at me. I said I'd been waiting for him, I'd been worried. He turned away and told me brusquely to stop, we weren't married.

I got up, put on my bathrobe, and went into the kitchen to do the dishes. When I came back, he was lying in bed reading a magazine. He asked whether he should go, and I shook my head. I sat on the bed and told him I liked him very much, and he said I should watch out that I didn't fall in love. He wasn't the right person for that. We kissed, and he pulled me back into bed.

In the early afternoon we drove out of the city. I brought along my cameras and the extra lenses.

At a village inn we had scrambled eggs and cheese. We were too late for lunch, and the owner served us very reluctantly.

Besides us there were only three old men in the restaurant. They watched us in silence and smoked. The entire time we were in the room they kept looking at us and didn't say a word. After he served us our food, the proprietor brought them beer and sat down at their table.

I said to Henry that the men were watching all our

movements closely. They've probably recognized us, I said, joking. Henry joined in. No wonder, he said, with those damned "Wanted" posters everywhere. He told me to keep an eye on the old men. He'd take care of the owner, maybe blow him away if he went for the phone. Then I'd have to hold off the old men while he made a run for the car.

Henry pulled his felt hat down over his brow. His eyes sparkled. What if the owner already phoned from the kitchen? I asked. Maybe the police were on their way.

That's possible, he whispered conspiratorially. But they'll never take me alive.

We nodded to each other with fierce determination.

Then the woman came in from the kitchen. She stood by our table and asked if we'd enjoyed the food. It really was pretty late, she said; otherwise she always served an excellent lunch. Did we come from Berlin? Did we know Choriner Strasse? That was where her daughter lived. She was married to a master baker and didn't miss the village at all.

When we asked for the bill, she said the boss took care of that. She called him over, and he grumpily accepted our money while she remained standing by the table. She wished us a good day and a pleasant drive.

As we were leaving, I turned toward the three old men. They stared at me without expression. I nodded to them, and they smiled back gratefully.

By now the ice cream stand next to the inn was open. Several young people with motorcycles were standing in front. Others were driving their bikes slowly around the group. They cut their engines and stared at us.

Two young girls were waiting by our car. They asked whether we could give them a lift. I asked where they wanted to go, and they said: Depends on where you're going. They grinned at me. I didn't understand what they wanted, and they laughed at me.

Then they went to the driver's side to ask Henry, who gave some answer I couldn't hear. The girls stuck their tongues out at him and called him an old faggot. Then they joined the group in front of the ice cream stand. They were maybe fifteen years old.

We got into the car. A boy yelled something at us, and the others laughed. He threw a handful of pebbles and sand at the windshield as Henry pulled away. Henry stopped the car instantly, but I begged him to drive on.

I asked what he'd said to the girls.

Nothing, he replied. Nothing special. Just that I wouldn't give them a lift.

I turned around and looked at the rapidly disappearing group with the motorcycles.

They're bored, I said.

Yes, Henry said, they're bored. They'll be bored all their lives.

I had the map out on my knees and was trying to settle on a destination. I chose a village that seemed to be on a river. The map showed a mill there, and I hoped it would be good to photograph.

Henry drove fast, as usual. While I was looking at the map, he described the canals in Amsterdam. He'd seen them as a child. In his dreams he often found himself standing by the canals. They must have made a deep impression on him.

There was a tractor ahead of us on the road. Then everything happened very fast. My head was still bent over the map, but I could feel that Henry had speeded up and pulled out of our lane to pass. When I looked up, the tractor was sideways to us. Henry hit the brakes, jerked the car to the left, accelerated, braked, and wrenched the steering wheel with both hands. I lunged forward in my seat belt, and braced myself against the windshield. For a moment one of the tractor's rear tires loomed in our right window. The car bounced and fell back. My head hit the roof, and I clung to Henry. The underside of the car or maybe the muffler scraped the road several times with a loud clang. The car lurched back and forth and finally slowed down. When Henry brought it to a stop, I looked for the tractor, which was now at right angles to the road. The driver was lying slumped over the huge steering wheel. All I could see was his back, without a head, and I must have cried out. Henry grabbed my arm and asked if I was all right. Without a word I pointed to the driver of the tractor. At that moment the man sat up, looked around, and climbed down from his high seat.

Another narrow escape, Henry said, and smiled at me reassuringly.

The car was in a potato field. It must have jumped the deep, narrow ditch that separated us from the road. I took a long breath and didn't respond.

The farmer had walked around his tractor, checking it. Now he came over to us. He pulled Henry's door open and shouted: Are you crazy? Didn't you see me? He kept on shouting.

Henry got out, glanced at the car, and asked the farmer whether there was any damage to his machine. The farmer continued shouting, saying he had had his signal on in plenty of time and had already been in the left lane when Henry tried to pass him. Henry asked him again whether the tractor was damaged. The farmer said no and grabbed Henry by the lapels. Didn't he understand that he'd come within a hair of killing us all? Crushing us like . . . he groped for a word, but none came to him.

Within a hair, Henry said mildly.

I couldn't see his face, but I could tell from his voice that he was smiling.

Within a hair, he repeated. Just think about everything that comes within a hair of happening.

The farmer let go of him, took a step backward. He stared at Henry in utter amazement.

I'll report you, he said hoarsely.

Then he raised his hand and hit Henry in the face. Henry stumbled backward and fell against the hood of the car, his head striking the metal. He lay still. His head was directly in front of me just a few inches away, separated from me only by the windshield. His eyes were closed. I jumped out of the car and grabbed him. He was unconscious.

Get some water! I yelled at the farmer. He stood pale and motionless by the car. I told him again to get water. I let Henry slide slowly to the ground. When I raised his head, he opened his eyes and looked at me. The farmer came clumping across the ditch. In his hand he had a bottle half full of some reddish soda.

Henry said everything was all right, and got up. He felt his left cheekbone. I said it would be better to lie down for a while, but he insisted we get moving right away.

The farmer, holding his bottle, stood indecisively by the car. His fury had dissipated, and he was muttering to himself.

I told him that everything was all right, he didn't have to stick around.

Really? he asked suspiciously.

He was about forty, but his stubble and slack chin made him look older.

It wouldn't have taken much, he said. Not much.

Henry was crouching behind the car examining the underside of the chassis.

Go on, I said. Just go, will you?

And since he was scratching his head uncertainly, I added, You don't need to worry—I'm a doctor.

That was a crazy thing to do, he said. It wouldn't have taken much.

He turned and ambled back to his tractor. Before starting up, he looked at us. He shook his head.

I climbed in behind the wheel. Henry observed me with narrowed eyes, but said nothing and got in the other side. I drove along the edge of the potato field until I found a crossing to the road. The tires dug into the soft earth.

Back on the highway, I asked Henry whether he hadn't noticed the tractor was turning left. He said he'd wanted to pass it before it turned. And then he added that he'd speeded up a second too late, a second in which he was thinking of me, thinking that driving fast made me uncomfortable. I didn't say anything; I was annoyed with myself for asking, and concentrated on driving well.

All that was left of the mill were fragments of walls and rotting beams. Apparently it had been stripped by the villagers. The place was overgrown with weeds. We had to make our way carefully so as not to stumble over pipes and pieces of iron hidden among the stinging nettles.

I photographed what was left of the roof, the caved-in rafters out of which a little birch was growing, with pale, almost colorless leaves. To reach it I had to scramble up what remained of the walls. Odds and ends were lying around on top—an old radio, rusty garden tools, a sawhorse, rotting, bubbly cardboard. Also earth, wisps of straw, and in the groove of an iron girder, a puddle of water with an oily violet film. I groped my way along a crumbling wall toward the skinny birch, no taller than a shrub, its twisted crown bent toward the outside, toward the open field, longing for the forest. My viewfinder captured the tree, a naked girder, the horizon. Then a baby carriage without wheels. I tried to edge further along. A stone gave way, something rolled down. Suddenly I broke out in a sweat. I reached for the wall and groped my way back. I didn't dare look around; I cursed my recklessness. Finally I got back to the piece of wall where I had begun to climb. Henry was waiting down below. He didn't notice me. He was poking at a thistle with the toe of his shoe. He seemed lost out here, with his shiny black shoes, his close-fitting vest, the felt hat. He stood there, bored, among the rank weeds, the tumbledown walls and rotting beams, the dark willows on the riverbank that were probably already dead; he looked as if he were at a party where he didn't know a soul and could barely hide his discomfort.

I called to him. He looked up and asked whether I had finished. Was he bored? I asked. He said it was bearable, and helped me climb down. He wanted to know what I'd photographed up there, but when I told him, he looked so baffled that I burst out laughing and gave him a hug.

Later we walked through the forest. Henry concentrated on avoiding the bushes and branches. It was obvious that he considered the walk an unnecessary ordeal. It meant nothing to him to stroll through the trees, feeling cushiony moss underfoot, or listen to the voices and noises of the

forest. The landscape didn't suit him, it impaired his movements. His face, his gestures showed annoyance at all its
details: the soft, swampy ground, the underbrush hung with
spider webs, the fallen branches crackling under our feet.
He was a city person. It meant nothing to him to be out
here. At first I kept talking, pointing things out, hopping
along ahead of him, determined not to take notice of his
boredom. When he stepped into a fox hole and swore, I
asked him what he had planned for Sunday. He was standing
on one leg, holding his ankle. Then he took a careful step,
limped, and answered that he planned to see his wife.

The reply took my breath away for a moment. I was
incapable of a single thought. My brain circled in a daze
around that word. I wanted to say something, some offhand
remark to prove that I was perfectly calm, and racked my
brains for one. Don't get so upset, I said to myself, don't
be such an idiot. But I could have howled with anger and
frustration. I felt humiliated, betrayed. He hadn't said a
thing to me. He'd never spoken of a wife, never said he was
married. And now this sudden piece of news. His wife. By
the way. He had a wife somewhere; also, he now volun-
teered, two children. I felt massively insulted. Why hadn't
he mentioned it? Why? And why did he bring it up now?

I walked on and on. I walked to keep myself from falling
down. The desire to be alone, to throw myself on the ground
and howl.

I didn't want to possess him. I never had any intention
of possessing him. I had decided long ago never to remarry,
never to give another person title to me. Our unspoken
agreement that neither would be responsible to the other
was something I took seriously. I was absolutely convinced
I had to maintain my distance from other people, in order

to avoid deception, in order to avoid deceiving. Yet—my constant readiness to abandon myself; my longing for infantile dependency. A dreary, sickly-sweet desire for security. Like the smell of flowers wilting on a casket, oppressive yet pleasant. I was armored against myself.

And now this surprise, so coolly given. The vague feeling of having been deceived again. A horror paralyzing my brain, taking my breath away. But why, why? I was nothing more than a casual affair for a married man. The same old ridiculous, banal situation, repeated a million times over. A pre-established pattern of escape. The standard method for avoiding obligation maintained in the higher interests of authority, untenable in thought, word, and deed.

I felt sick. My face was burning with shame. I rushed on through the woods, branches lashing against my knees, my face. I could feel my heart pounding. Then Henry's footsteps coming closer. Suddenly in front of me an adder quickly slithered from a stone into the bushes. I stopped short, fell down, cursed my high heels. I scrambled to my feet and hobbled on. Henry's hand grabbed my arm, jerked me around. Why are you running, he panted, what's wrong? He reached for my face, and I backed away. His right eye was almost swollen shut, the skin above his cheekbone black and blue. The swelling distorted his face. A grotesque mask shouting at me.

He stood before me, gasping for air. He tried to catch his breath. His head heaved as he coughed. Meanwhile he stared at me numbly. Why are you laughing? he asked. He shook my arm. Why are you laughing? He held me so tightly that it hurt. Your eye, was all I could say, and only then did I notice that I was laughing loudly, hysterically. I was shaking with laughter. Why stop now, I thought, and went on laughing, on and on. I felt my throat tightening, cutting off my breath. You'll laugh yourself hoarse, I found myself thinking. I tried to go on walking. He held me with both hands and shook me, pulled at me. Go ahead and hit me, I thought, you want to, you need to. Why are you laughing? he hissed angrily. I tore away and ran on. He seized me by the shoulder, threw himself on me, and we fell to the damp ground. I felt my back hit something hard, maybe a tree root. Or rubble. He tore at my clothes, and I clung to him. His mouth was near my ear. He was panting. Again: Why are you laughing? He pushed up my dress, tugged at my underwear. I dug my fingers into his neck. Before my eyes a tree limb danced, with dull, lusterless leaves. I felt tears running into my ear. And still that limb, a pale leaf-green, dotted with light and the brownish shadows of the forest. Shadows and light, brightness, darkness, foreground, background, the coolness of the earth, the tree root scraping away at my spine. No, I thought, no. Then my anger melted away, my despair. Melted, or merged with a sudden surge of desire, with the dancing leaves, with Henry's panting breath, with the feeling of ultimate solitude.

We lay next to each other without moving, wordless, half naked. For some reason I wondered where the car was. But it didn't interest me. It was quiet in the forest. I kept my eyes closed. Bright veils of light shone through my lids. I didn't want to see him or answer his questions, didn't want to have to explain something I couldn't explain. What could I say? I didn't even understand myself.

At some point we returned to the car and drove home. I was freezing and shivered uncontrollably. Since I didn't say anything, Henry turned on the radio.

We got back to Berlin around ten o'clock. Henry walked me to the door of my apartment. We both avoided speaking. He said good-bye almost politely, and I gave him a friendly smile. A kiss on the forehead. See you soon. Sleep well. I closed the door quickly behind me.

Later I wrote a letter to my sister. Then I tore it up. Before I went to bed I took a tranquilizer. Not unusual for me. Even so I lay awake a long time. I was annoyed with myself. I turned on the television and stared at the bright, blank screen for several minutes. Then I leafed through the biography of a musician and thought about having a drink. In the refrigerator I found an open bottle of vodka and poured myself a big glass. I put it on the bedside table. It smelled and tasted disgusting. I drank and stared at the ceiling. It was a little past two, and I heard the elevator moving. I said to myself, You've cried a little, now just let it be. Let's go to sleep. You want to be a big girl, don't you? No Mama, I don't. I don't want to be a big girl. But you still have so much ahead of you. I don't want to, Mama, I don't want to.

6

. . . .

At the end of June I took my vacation. As usual I went to
the beach. I had suggested to Henry that we take separate
vacations. Temporary solitude, a break from obligations, a
vacation from reality. Probably also an unacknowledged fear
of too much intimacy, of the inevitable loss of distance that
living together every day and every hour for several weeks

would bring. The idea of having to be considerate of another person twenty-four hours a day was intolerable to me. As was the thought that someone else might have to tolerate my foibles.

Henry had agreed immediately. He even seemed relieved.

On the day of my departure, he went to work two hours late so he could carry my suitcase to the car. We went to the café across the street. He held my hand and looked at me in silence. At the table next to us sat two women, both in their mid-forties, both with dyed hair, blonde and strawberry-blonde.

Blonde was holding a ring and a necklace in her open right hand; she kept picking them up absentmindedly with her other hand, then letting them fall back into her palm. Tears were streaming down her face, smearing the heavy make-up. She was crying almost without a sound. All you could hear was a soft, high-pitched whine.

Strawberry-Blonde talked to her insistently, tossing out short sentences and then gazing at her friend dully, her chin sagging helplessly. Blonde didn't react at all. Strawberry-Blonde was saying that somebody was a brutal bastard who deserved a kick in the balls. Then she asked what he'd said. When she got no reply, her chin went slack again. Her black skirt had ridden up. She was sweating. She finished her schnapps and said, He doesn't have any earlobes. People like that are always bad.

I smiled. I knew this game.

Blonde slowly shook her head. Without taking her eyes off the jewelry in her hand, she said, No, he's not bad. Just young.

Her friend looked dissatisfied but didn't contradict her.

They both fell silent. Then Strawberry-Blonde insisted: But he must have said something.

Blonde didn't answer, just went on crying softly.

Henry nudged me. He laid his hand on my belly and said he wanted to go to bed with me. I pushed his hand away and said I had to get going. I wanted to be at the ocean before the midday heat. I paid, and we got up.

As we were leaving, I turned around to look at the two women. Blonde was wearing a large red paste butterfly in her hair. It was dangling from a strand by her right eye: hope glittering in her unhappiness, this laughing, laughable butterfly sparkling on her puffy face.

At the car we kissed. With his hands in his vest pockets, he watched me drive away.

As I did every year, I spent my vacation in a village on the Achterwasser, near the Bay of Pomerania. I stayed with a farm family. In the village I passed for the wife's cousin: no one was permitted to take in vacationers. I had a room on the second floor, a garret with a bed and a wardrobe. There was no armchair, in fact no chair at all, but that didn't bother me. On vacation I went to bed early.

Sometimes I spent the evening with Gertrud and Jochen, my hosts. They like to talk about their children, two girls. The younger one is a cook in the district capital, the older one was married last fall and lives in the next village. The wedding cost twelve thousand marks, and the guests had to be driven to the church in two buses. Gertrud and Jochen talk a lot about the wedding.

Usually I'm already in bed when they come in. In addition to their work on the collective farm, they have their own animals—cows, pigs, hens. This means they have to get up at five every day and work until eight in the evening. I think they do it for the money, but I'm not sure. Maybe they can't imagine any other way to live. I asked them once, but they either didn't understand my question or didn't want to talk about it with me. It's their own business, after all; they don't have to tell me anything. Also it really doesn't interest me. Probably I asked them because what they were doing seemed absurd to me. But they're content, and sometimes I envy them. In a way it's a nice form of craziness to work so hard and then spend so much money on a daughter's wedding. Anyhow, they enjoy it and wouldn't want it any other way.

In the past I occasionally helped out in the barn. I tossed bales of straw down from the loft or cut up old bread for the hens. I also helped Gertrud clip the hens' wings. But the two of them don't like me to help. Jochen said they could manage the work fine by themselves, and I was here to rest. So in the evening I simply make myself supper in the kitchen and then go up to my room. I read a little, but soon fall asleep. The sea air makes me tired.

During the day I lie on the beach. Since there are only a few vacationers in the village—relatives or pseudo-relatives like me—it's quiet by the water. Usually I'm the only one there. A few teenagers from the village regularly show up on their bikes and motorcycles. They stop at a distance, and look at me. After a while they ride away, but eventually they come back.

When I first stayed in the village I used to sunbathe without a suit. Probably they were hoping to catch me naked again. School vacation is so long, they have nothing to do, and I was their only form of excitement. I would have liked to go on sunbathing naked, but it might have caused trouble, and I wanted to spare my hosts.

I sent Henry two postcards, meaningless comments about commonplace feelings. Stupid remarks which made even me uncomfortable. I didn't feel capable of really telling him anything. The postcards themselves paralyze me. The carefully allotted space for a personal message compressed into illiterate three-word sentences. Then the retouched photographs imposing themselves on both sender and message. Sometimes even a prefabricated greeting, a bold expression of cordiality. Of course I could have written him letters, but I had nothing to say.

That I was longing for him. Yearning. A word too imprecise to describe the simple wish that occasionally came over me. Yearning spins a web of feeling to span the distance between us. A web to catch the victims of solitude, to keep them glued and pinned.

On the second weekend I drove to a nearby village. I'd been invited to the summer house of a dentist who works at the Charité Hospital in Berlin. I met him here years ago, him and his present wife. In Berlin we call each other occasionally, even talk about getting together, but in the end we only see each other here.

Fred was standing in the doorway when I got out of the car. We kissed and went into the house. We had an aperitif and assured ourselves that we were looking splendid. He talked loudly and seemed in a good mood. When he offered me a refill, I refused.

He talked incessantly. Maybe he was happy I had come, maybe he was just restless. He drank a good deal and told me about the house, about repairing the roof: I paid for twenty bundles of reeds. They brought me twelve. They say it was a bad winter. You know, they don't cut the reeds unless the seawater freezes over. I went along once. With a sickle, cutting close to the ice. If it doesn't freeze, they don't go out cutting.

He lay on the sofa, his legs draped over my chair, and continually massaged his fingers: Besides, nobody does that anymore. Just a few old people. And everything they bring back is snapped up in no time. You can't beat a thatched roof.

He poked me with the tip of his shoe: Still flying solo?

I was flustered, his question took me by surprise. I said, Yes, then added quickly, More or less.

He laughed like a goat and said contentedly, I understand. He leered at me, his eyes oozing assumed collusion.

More or less, he repeated to himself. Then he drained his glass and went back to talking about the house.

Later Maria came in. She went right to the sideboard and poured herself a glass of schnapps. We said nothing, just watched. Then Fred said nervously, Claudia's here.

Maria turned to me, nodded, and muttered a greeting. She left the room with her glass in hand. Fred closed his eyes and said wearily: She's pretty silly—more or less.

I laughed, but didn't know why.

Maria's his third wife. Like her predecessors, she started out as his receptionist, and now she suspects him of cheating on her with the new one. At least that's what Fred claimed.

We ate lunch in the kitchen, a large room with a huge window and farm furniture, or what people nowadays call farm furniture. Here in the village, of course, none of the farmers have it. The chairs look rickety, and they're not very comfortable.

We had fish filet and fried potatoes, both from the freezer. Maria didn't eat anything. She sat at the table, smoking one cigarette after the other, and watched us.

Tell me something, she urged me. Tell me a joke or something.

Yes, tell her a joke, Fred said in a friendly way, and then explain it to her.

Maria stared at her cigarette without expression. She didn't seem to be listening. Her face was pale and tired. Maybe she was on drugs. When she saw me looking at her, she ran her hand through her reddish hair and smiled. I was struck by her fingernails, patches of chipped red on gnawed-off gray horn. I remembered how in school, when I was sixteen or seventeen, I classified people by their earlobes and fingernails. A fiendish code of judgment which I used to reward my girlfriends or drive them to tears. A game I then fell prey to myself, helplessly stuck in the grip of rules that defied all logic and experience. And with the self-righteousness and arrogance of that age, I made firm resolutions, irrevocable decisions, and so ordered my little world. A stupid, nasty game, and what a mess it made.

Maria's dirty, childish fingernails. I felt an urge to push back her hair so I could check her earlobes.

Fred noticed I was looking at her. He went over to her, pressed his middle finger against her right cheekbone, and with his index finger pulled down her eyelid. He smiled at me and said: See, a well-developed narcissistic hypochondria. I would almost call it classic.

Pig, Maria said quietly. She sat motionless without pushing him away.

Fred didn't allow himself to be interrupted: In addition, a tendency toward hysteria, as a result of repressed instincts and unassimilated outside stimuli. You have to understand that she's suffering. She's misunderstood, oppressed, castrated. She read somewhere that the modern, self-aware woman has to be unhappy, and she wants to be a modern, self-aware woman too. So she suffers from depression. My God, how depressive she is. And of course I'm the one who's to blame for the whole misery: the man, the monster, the patriarchal tyrant. Constantly forcing his will and his penis on her. A systemic neurosis: Destroy that which is destroying you, and so on. She keeps a big kitchen knife under her pillow so she can cut off my balls in case my masculine perversity should give me the urge to screw her. As her husband and doctor, I can diagnose two delayed reactions: First, her culinary ability, which was never very impressive, is going downhill at breakneck speed. Second, her idiocy is increasing proportionally. She's going insane. As a doctor I give her at most two years; as a husband I'm less optimistic.

Fred rubbed her cheek playfully. Maria stared at her cigarette. She didn't react to him. I said I wanted to go and lie down, and got to my feet.

Fred blocked my way: Did I already mention that she lets any guy who comes along fuck her? I caught her one time. I came home, and wowee . . .

I pushed him aside and went up to my room. I tried to sleep, but I kept thinking of Maria's pale, narrow face. I asked myself why I'd come. From my earlier visits I knew all about their fighting. Why did I subject myself year after year to his tirades and her despair, these mutual bonds which kept them hopelessly enfettered.

When I woke up, Fred was standing by my bed. He said Henry had come. At first I didn't understand, I was too sleepy and surprised. What Fred actually said was that my "more or less" was downstairs, and it took me a while to realize he meant Henry. I asked him to say that I'd be right down, but he stayed by the bed. I said I wanted to get dressed and he should leave. He gave a silly laugh, and started handing me my underthings. For a moment we looked at each other without speaking. I knew the game he was playing: I was supposed to beg him to leave the room. He would refuse. I was supposed to get angry, yell and shout until Maria or Henry came into the room. Then he would act the man of the world who had frightened this timid little creature. He would treat it as a joke designed to demonstrate the extent of my sexual repression. He would make a big show of feeling sorry for Henry, and would go on about it all evening, long after anyone else wanted to listen. It was another of his parlor games. I think he calls them "applied psychoanalysis." As he says, a human being stripped of all the compulsions and concealments that we call civilized behavior is simply a set of well functioning genitalia, which, when finally liberated, provides an orgiastic release for all other human needs, and so asserts its own force as irrefutable, all-powerful. Occasionally he gives this game a simpler label: a journey into the human interior, or a visit to the wild beast, the swine within. The game had many variations. And his horrible whims and the tears or outbursts he provoked, all the little humiliations, were merely devices to keep his boredom at bay.

All right, I said, threw back the covers, and got up. I put on my clothes, trying not to hurry too obviously or show any discomfort. I acted as if I didn't hear his remarks about my breasts and hips. It wasn't that hard to shut them out—the blood was pounding in my ears.

Henry was sitting in the kitchen. He had appeared at

Gertrud and Jochen's shortly after I left, and they had given
him directions for finding me. He hadn't said anything to
me beforehand, he wanted to surprise me.

Henry and I had a cup of coffee with Maria and then
went down to the beach. It was cool and windy. The town's
main street was crowded with people. Ahead of us vacationers tramped along, swathed in glowing slickers. On the
other side of the street, more vacationers in the same yellow
raingear. Like the uniforms worn by inmates of institutions.

Henry asked about Fred and Maria—were they friends of
mine? I said I'd known them for a few years and didn't see
them often. I wouldn't say they were friends.

We walked along close to the water. The waves had
washed up a broad border of gray-white foam. The wind
was gusty, which I enjoyed. We saw only a few other beach-
combers. The wicker huts lined up close together were
deserted and locked.

We talked about friends, and I said I wasn't sure whether
I had any. When I was young, I had a girlfriend in the small
town where I grew up. I wore my hair in pigtails, and swore
eternal friendship with her, and I suppose back then we
really were friends. But that was so long ago, I said, and
probably too childish to mention. Today I wouldn't be able
to say what a friend was. Maybe I was no longer ready or
able to commit myself to another person, which was an
obvious prerequisite for this strange thing called friendship.
I probably didn't need friends. I had acquaintances, good
acquaintances; I saw them occasionally, and I enjoyed their
company. But in reality they were interchangeable, and
therefore not essential to me. I liked being with people; I
found many of them interesting, and it gave me pleasure
to talk to them. But that was about it. Sometimes I felt a

vague yearning for something like a friend, a pale little school friend, but it didn't come very often; it was like crying, in spite of myself, over some sentimental movie. It wasn't real sadness. Yes, that's how it is, I said.

Henry had listened without interrupting. Now we walked along the beach in silence. It looked dirty and neglected. There were no more walkers or beach huts in sight. My face was burning from the wind and the little grains of sand. We had taken off our shoes. Our feet were cold, but it was easier to walk that way.

Henry wanted to know what it had been like. I asked what he meant, and he said: Back then, where you grew up. I said I only had vague memories and wasn't sure how much they'd been falsified by time. I think I was different then, I said.

I certainly had hopes, and must have had something like plans and a clear notion of what life should be like. But even in those days I was afraid. And maybe I never was any different, and maybe that was just the beginning of all this.

Henry didn't say anything. We kept walking along the beach. We picked up shells, and Henry asked whether I wanted to go swimming with him. I refused; it was too cold. Henry quickly slipped out of his clothes and ran into the waves. He plunged headfirst into the water. He swam rapidly, with flailing movements. He yelled something I couldn't make out. When he came out of the water, he was shivering. I rubbed him vigorously with my sweater, and we laughed at his penis, which was all shriveled up from the cold. Then we ran the whole way back, and arrived panting and out of breath at Maria's.

That evening, some of Fred's friends who were vacationing nearby came over. Everybody tried to act very relaxed;

people told jokes and drank a lot of wine and schnapps.
Maria said almost nothing the entire evening, but no one
noticed. Henry and I wanted to get to bed early, the walk
on the beach had tired us out. When we were about to go
up to our room, Fred stopped us, saying he was giving this
party in our honor. He kept at us until we gave in and
stayed downstairs.

A painter, who was there with an unusually beautiful
girl, was talking about art.

We're nothing but voyeurs, he said, and only if we're
voyeurs are we artists. Any other kind of art is finished,
dead and gone, bourgeois crap. The only worthwhile object
for art is the antisocial element, the marginal human being.
For hundreds of years art concerned itself with the opinions
and problems of the petty bourgeoisie. Sugary dinner music
to help parasites digest their precious spiritual aches and
pains. But art is anarchy. Art is the scourge of society. The
only valid aesthetic principle is shock; the measure of all
true art is the piercing scream. We must become antisocial
in order to recognize what we are, where we come from,
where we're going. Filth, that's my message to you.

The beautiful girl stroked his head and laughed at him
when he looked at her. He was annoyed that no one contradicted him. His voice got louder and louder, and he
swore at Fred, who was trying to calm him down. Somehow
they smoothed things over and toasted their friendship.

I sat down by the fireplace and stared into the flames.
My face was pleasantly flushed. One of Fred's friends came
and sat beside me. He offered me a cigarette and talked
about the dying oceans, the greenhouse effect, and the impact of the energy shortage on the Latin American economy.
He said he was a professor of pluromedial aesthetics and

communications, and lived in Bochum, in the West. I was amazed. I couldn't form a very clear picture of his field; I would have thought he was a salesman or a grade school teacher. He asked me about my work and then talked about acupuncture. He was maybe thirty-five, had good, even teeth, and was self-assured in an agreeable way. I was irritated by his constant, ingratiating smile. It was as if he wanted to persuade me to buy something at a good price.

When Henry came over, the West German introduced himself very formally. He handed us his card and said what good company we were. He insisted that we call him Horst and assured us that he liked everything here. He said that politically he was a moderate leftist and didn't think much of the capitalist system. On the other hand, he couldn't help noticing all the mistakes we were making here. Then he wanted to know what Henry thought about the German Question. Henry said he'd been running around on the beach all day and was covered with sand. He absolutely had to wash his hair. Horst had a good laugh at that and said Henry was terrific, he understood just what he meant. Then he wanted to know what Henry did. I got up and went into the kitchen.

Maria was there fixing ice cream and coffee. I wanted to help, and she had me rinse the glasses. I asked her about various guests, but she didn't know them. Fred always invited lots of people over because he was bored here, she said. Later they might see each other again on the beach, but that was all. The painter was the only one who came often. Maria said he was an impractical person; everything that could go wrong for him did. He kept dropping things and breaking them. She told me some stories about him, and we laughed a lot. We were getting along well.

Fred poked his head into the kitchen. He wanted to know what we were talking about. Maria said he should take the coffee and ice cream into the living room. She sat down, lit a cigarette, and watched me as I dried the glasses.

Have you noticed? she asked. Her voice was brittle.

What? I asked. What was I supposed to have noticed?

My face, she said. Look at me, look at my face.

I smiled at her. All right, I see it. There's nothing wrong, Maria.

Her eyes turned glassy. She didn't believe me.

There's nothing wrong, I repeated. You look fine.

She shook her head slowly and energetically without taking her eyes off me.

No, she said, you have to see it, because I can see it myself.

What am I supposed to see?

I don't know, she said, and fell silent. She didn't trust me. I waited. That seemed best. I heard dance music from the living room. Maria sat with her head bowed and puffed violently on her cigarette.

It's just that I think I'm losing weight, she began softly. My bones are starting to show. Doesn't this look like a skull?

Again she offered me her face for inspection. She smiled sadly, and her gentle manner showed that she was more than sad. She was desperate.

You're talking yourself into something, Maria; everything's all right. Now I was using that tone of mine I so despise. It was the doctor talking, that soothing, omnipotent voice. The kindergarten manner. An occupational disease one acquires from dealing with patients; the entire hospital down to the youngest nurse talks that way. Kind and soothing, everything will be all right. The mask of our helplessness.

You know, Maria said, every morning whole bunches of hair come off in my comb.

That's perfectly normal, I said.

She shook her head. That much isn't normal, you don't have to hide the truth from me.

Don't talk yourself into something. You'll drive yourself crazy. It's perfectly normal. Everyone loses bunches of hair every day. And your face is fine. You were always pale. And it suits you, you know that.

Fred says so too.

What does Fred say too?

That I'm crazy.

I got really angry. She just sat there, her eyes closed, obviously suffering. But why did she have to tell me these things? Why are these sensitive souls so unbelievably insensitive when it comes to someone other than themselves?

Listen, I said, you know perfectly well I didn't mean it that way. Why the hell are you insinuating that I . . .

She wasn't listening. She puffed distractedly on her cigarette and drew on the plastic tablecloth with her finger.

Why don't you leave Fred? I asked. Maybe that's your problem.

That's none of your business, she said, and continued to trace invisible loops on the tablecloth. I went on drying glasses, putting them away.

Suddenly Maria said, It's deeper than that, much deeper. Something that happened long ago.

I felt the need to touch her, and stroked her face. She

kissed my hand lightly and leaned against my arm. And then we put our heads together and giggled like two little girls.

Maria said she was tired and wanted to go to bed. I went back into the living room. Henry was still sitting by the fire with Horst. I came up behind him and whispered that we should slip away. Henry nodded, relieved. The professor from the West was holding forth on the eco-freaks' critique of immanence. I asked Henry what he meant. He said he didn't know, he'd been listening but not following. Horst seemed hurt. He tried to explain it to us, but gave up after a little while when he saw we weren't interested. Without transition he started to talk about the breakdown of the German language and the proliferation of Americanisms. Apparently he could expound on any subject. He reminded me of a comic-strip character, filling up little balloons with speech and then sending them sailing off into the air.

Henry said, Horst talks so he won't be left alone with himself for a minute.

The West German gave a nervous laugh. Then he remarked that everything here was like the nineteenth century, marvellously intact, like a forgotten village. Like some country invented by Adalbert Stifter. I said I had never read anything by Stifter.

You don't have to read it, Horst said, you're living it.

When we said good-bye to Horst he mentioned again what good company we were, and said it would be nice if we could meet again. We both agreed we would find it nice too and left the room. He was still flashing that ingratiating smile. I think he was very lonely.

Out in the hallway some of the guests were shooting an air gun at lighted candles on a stool outside the bathroom door. Some pellets had already lodged in the enameled door, and the rippled opaque glass in the little window had webs of hairline cracks where it had been hit. From the bathroom a woman's voice could be heard whining, pleading to be let out, which seemed to amuse the shooters.

Fred and the painter were sitting on the sofa, the beautiful girl between them. Fred had his head against her neck and was stroking her breasts, and the painter was sobbing to himself, moaning how he had betrayed art, betrayed himself. While speaking these words, he clapped his hands melodramatically.

When we walked past them, the girl nodded at us. At the door to our room we could still hear the painter accusing himself.

It was almost noon when we woke up. All was quiet in the house. The sun was high in a brilliantly clear, icy-blue sky. The wind had died down. Children's voices wafted in through the window. Henry suggested we go swimming. I put on my nightgown and went down to fetch bathrobes for us.

Maria was already up, reading. The beautiful girl from last night was fussing around in the kitchen. She had slept on the sofa. Maria gave me the bathrobes and told me about a shortcut to the ocean.

The beach was crowded. We walked for a long time until we found a quieter spot. The water was cold, and at first we swam fast and got out of breath. The cold burned our skin. Soon Henry wanted to turn back, but I asked him to stay in with me a little longer. He swam up and wound his legs around me. We kissed and swallowed water. I dunked his head and swam away. He had trouble catching up. On the beach we rubbed each other down and hopped around on one leg to shake the water out of our ears. Then we wrapped ourselves in the bathrobes and ran back to the house.

Maria or the girl had made coffee and eggs for us, and we sat down at the table in our bathrobes and had breakfast. The girl told us she spent the whole summer at the ocean. She didn't have a place to stay, but so far she had always found someone to take her in. She asked whether she could spend a few nights with me, but I explained that I only had one tiny room. I said I was sorry, but the girl laughed and told me not to worry about it.

I said to Henry that she was a very beautiful girl, didn't he think so too? He nodded and said yes, blushing. The girl laughed again, and Henry was annoyed. He said I was beautiful too. And Maria as well; she too was a very beautiful woman. Maria looked at me. I knew what she was thinking, and although I hadn't told Henry anything about our conversation, her suspicion hurt me. For a moment I considered clearing up the misunderstanding. But what could I say? I gave up the idea.

For some reason, some lines of a poem from school came into my head. I had read them years ago, or heard them on the radio, and I didn't know why they returned to me just then: When the moment calls for Great Deeds, we can only stir our coffee vigorously, almost with integrity.

That was how it went, or something like that. I thought I'd forgotten it, yet bits of the poem had survived somewhere in my memory. I couldn't even say that the lines had any special meaning for me. No one is calling on me to perform any great deeds; those are just dreams, schoolday dreams, my little school poet. The hopes and delusions of a skinny little girl with pigtails. What remains are a few habits, some vague yearnings, a slight, persistent headache, and now and then a misunderstanding that can't be cleared up. Another reason to stir vigorously, almost with integrity.

In the ensuing pause the beautiful blonde girl remarked: It certainly got quiet all of a sudden. She laughed.

We soon said good-bye. I gave Maria a kiss on the cheek, which she accepted passively and indifferently. Fred wasn't up yet, so I asked her to say good-bye to him for us. She nodded, but I wasn't sure she'd heard me. I was already sitting in the car when the beautiful girl—her name was Helga—called from the window that I should wait. She came running out and gave me a large, pale-green apple. All out of breath, she said, I wanted to give you something. This is all I have.

Her hand was on the open window of the car. I could see her face with the sun directly behind it, and it looked unreal, transparent. For a moment I placed my hand on hers.

Thank you, and all the best, I said.

She laughed again. I quickly put on my sunglasses.

Henry followed me in his car. I stopped in my village, but then drove on, down to the water. We lay in the grass along the beach. In the afternoon we opened some cans Henry had brought along. We ate cold soup and meat dumplings, after removing the layer of congealed fat on top.

We soon ran out of cigarettes, but we were tired and neither of us wanted to drive into town. We fell asleep on the warm, coarse grass. At some point, children from the village woke us up. In the afternoon it rained, and we sat in Henry's car. The world disappeared behind the raindrops bursting against the windshield. We sat there, in the car, enclosed by the water streaming down the windows. Two survivors at the bottom of the sea. The music on the radio hardly got through to us. Last signals from a distant civilization that the flood might already have washed away.

Later the rain let up, but the sun stayed behind clouds. It had turned cool. In the evening the wind rose and blackened the water. The damp forest earth stuck to our shoes, and the leaves showered us with water.

I urged Henry to go back to Berlin. As we said goodbye, I asked him not to turn up again without letting me know, either here or in Berlin. He nodded and asked whether it had been so awful.

No, I said, it was lovely that you came. But I don't like to be surprised. I don't want to be caught unaware, not even by you.

We kissed each other, and he drove off. I followed him until the taillights of his car disappeared. Then I got into my car and went back to the village.

Gertrud and Jochen asked whether Henry had found me. I said yes, and made myself some supper. Then I joined them in front of the television. Jochen offered me a beer, and I smoked a cigarette, the first in hours. Somehow I felt drained, and very relieved.

7

. . . .

Some annoying things happened at the hospital after my vacation. I even wrote a letter of resignation, but withdrew it after a talk with the chief.

The doctor who covered for me while I was away had undermined my patients' confidence in me. He suggested to some of them that they switch doctors; with others he questioned my diagnoses. He stopped or changed treatments I had ordered. Of course he did it all very subtly and by innuendo, but I could sense that some of my patients no longer trusted me. Besides, Carla told me the whole story on my first day back. She put on a show of indignation, but she'd obviously enjoyed the intrigue. I know my Carla.

I called up the other doctor and told him what I thought of his methods. He was very rude, and I hung up. I considered asking for a disciplinary hearing. But I decided against it. It would only bring about interminable discussions, and in the end the professional verdict would pronounce both treatments to be correct. We would both be reprimanded and told to show more collegial spirit. So I resigned.

I didn't exactly mean to leave; I just wanted to register a protest against such shabby behavior. The chief called me up. Would I have time for him Thursday evening? Why didn't I come to his house?

I bought a bunch of roses for his wife, and braced myself for being yelled at or else coaxed and flattered into staying.

It was the first time I'd ever gone to his home. He lived in one half of a two-family house on the southern edge of the city. There was an intercom at the front gate, which seemed odd to me, since the house was only a few steps away. The chief opened the door. He greeted me by brushing my hand with his lips, and called me "dear child." This stupid address reassured me: there'd be no yelling today.

He introduced me to his wife, a worn, timid person in an apron. I would have taken her for the maid.

For dinner we had filet of pork, asparagus, a white Bordeaux, and then cake. He talked about the latest escape: a senior physician had defected to Bavaria. Then he talked about a scandal involving an American medical journal. A charlatan had palmed off faked data on the well-respected publication. The old man told the story with gusto, dwelling on the specifics of the case. His wife didn't say much, but it was obvious she worshipped him. She urged me to take a look at her husband's library in the next room. It had thousands of books, she said. Her husband read all the professional literature, in every language. She even said: He reads all languages, English and everything.

Her husband told her to shut up, and she fell silent without resentment. Later he sent her out of the room to make coffee. Then he talked about my resignation. He remained friendly, and spoke in his dear-child tone, but left no doubt as to his view of the situation. He impressed me. I liked his decisiveness, his self-satisfied, robust views. Certainly he's no noble soul, and even a bit naïve, but he radiates a sense of balance. I envied him. Nonetheless I knew my jealousy was mixed with too much arrogance for him to really get to me.

He said he wouldn't accept my resignation. I had reacted hysterically. If I wanted to leave, fine, I'd be doing the other doctor a favor. Maybe that's what he wanted all along; maybe he had my job in mind for a friend of his.

I enjoyed listening. The chief would make a good grandfather. In the end I promised to withdraw my resignation.

Later his wife joined us, still wearing her apron. She said they seldom had company, the children and many of her old friends were in West Germany. Actually all she had was her husband. She looked at him admiringly and humbly. He mumbled something and brushed the ashes off his vest. As I was leaving, she invited me to come again soon. Then she looked at her husband and said, Isn't that right, darling?

He stood broad and self-confident in the doorway and smiled at her. Then he closed his eyes and said, We're old people, Mother.

It was a tender and crazily comical scene, my boss in his pinstripe suit, vest, and silver-gray tie, a smoldering cigar in his hand, calling the washed-out little housewife beside him "Mother."

I saw Henry regularly, two or three times a week. He usually came for supper; we didn't go out often. I was tired and didn't want to leave the apartment. After a vacation, work tires me even more. I'm not good at adjusting to new things: the first week of vacation also makes me jittery. I can't stand interruptions in my daily rhythm. Maybe I shouldn't take a vacation; after all, people didn't take them in the nineteenth century. At any rate, a vacation is only partly restful for me.

I usually spend my weekends alone. Henry agreed to that. I need the two days for myself, to fritter away by myself, without having to think about anyone else's needs. Besides, I'm often on call on Sundays. And every two or three weeks Henry visits his wife and the children. He shouldn't feel that he has to decide between them and me.

His wife lives in Dresden. She's a chemist at the Technical University. A few years after getting his degree, Henry moved back to Berlin. At first he hoped to find a position for his wife here, but after two years they had both gotten used to being apart. She has a live-in boyfriend, and everyone concerned accepts the situation. No one's thinking of a divorce. As Henry says, they've never discussed it. Probably neither of them would want to marry again, and for the sake of the children they keep up a sort of friendship. I like her attitude. Why should they get the state involved in

something that only concerns them? My divorce was unpleasant enough. What gives some agency the right to poke
around in the private lives of two people? Three men and
a woman sitting behind a table. I found their questions
humiliating. Officially sanctioned peeping Toms, with no
sense of shame. My husband and I didn't want to live
together any more, that was all. We were reprimanded
several times. We stood before them like petty criminals,
like shoplifters. Helpless. Of course they did succeed in
making me feel guilty.

The wedding had also been a farce. A woman we didn't
know, perspiring in her suit; admonitions, obligations,
homilies praising the miracle of love. Prepackaged sentences
poured out of little foil pouches. Finally the contract. Sig-
natures, financial statements, a transfer. I laughed out of
sheer embarrassment. When I look at our wedding photo,
I don't recognize myself. A pale, immature face next to an
adolescent-looking young man. Surrounded by beaming relatives whose joyful relief leaps out of the picture. Two
helpless creatures, interchangeable right down to the pose
and the position of their heads. Only much later, looking
at other wedding pictures, did I discover the anarchists
lurking behind those submissive faces. Confused, nervous
revolutionaries, but in their eyes gleams some of the happiness and hope common to all anarchy. They want to flee,
destroy, reform the oppressive circumstances that encircle
them so arrogantly in the picture. And the only conceivable
alternative entangles them helplessly in the old intolerable
situation. Their day of revolt is already their end. But for
the moment the humiliations, the intrusive signs of defeat—
marriage contract, signature, group photo—are blithely
overlooked. Welcome to the bosom of our shared past, make

yourself at home in the innocent chokehold. And all shall be as it was: in order.

On the first weekend in August I developed all the film that had accumulated and made some enlargements. I enjoyed doing it, but it's so much trouble that I only get around to it twice a year at most. The kitchen and bathroom become a darkroom. I have to eat at the restaurant around the corner. This time I had almost thirty rolls of film to develop. Once I had seventy-three, which kept me working day and night.

The basins with developer and fixer go on the kitchen table, the enlarger on the stove, fastened down with clamps. I put the finished pictures in a pail and carry them to the shower stall to soak.

Almost all the pictures were taken in Brandenburg; three rolls were from the Achterwasser. Mother asked me once why I photographed only landscapes—trees, paths, rocks, tumbledown houses, lifeless wood. At the time her question perplexed me. I didn't know why; I couldn't give her an answer. I hadn't even realized that I never photographed people. Thinking it over later, I could hardly explain it to myself. I guess photographing people strikes me as a form of indiscreet prying into their lives. The idea that I could capture anyone in a picture is silly anyway. Somewhere I read that there are primitive peoples who have religious prohibitions against being photographed. (It amazed me to find that one of my own attitudes might be based on religious motives. Strangely, I had already discovered that certain religions shared other attitudes of mine. Yet questions of faith and transcendence never meant anything to me. I never related to those things, never gave them any thought.

When I was a child they preoccupied me for a time. But later not at all.)

It upsets me to see the unnatural poses people strike in pictures. Trees stay the way they are; they don't try to look better for the camera. Anyhow, I'm only interested in lines, horizons, perspective, the simple givens of nature and anything nature has reclaimed.

Anyway, it's just something I do now and then. Weeks can pass without my taking any pictures, and I don't miss it.

Although there are only a few negatives that I enlarge and print, five whole compartments in my armoire are already stuffed with pictures. I don't plan on doing anything with them. I don't want to put them on display, nor do I show them to anybody. I really don't know what the point of the whole thing is. I don't ask myself questions like that, I couldn't possibly answer them. I'm afraid they might call my "self" into question. Besides, this kind of introspection leaves me cold. I know some people are surprised at that and don't want to believe me, but that's how it is. I'm satisfied with it. I don't feel any need to delve into the so-called mysteries of life. The reproach that I exist unconsciously, like an animal—I think it was a fellow student who once said that—doesn't faze me. I'm just not cut out for any kind of mysticism. And I consider mystical any set of ideas that tries to express something beyond what biology can confirm. I don't need it. I feel that's one of my strengths.

I like those moments in the darkroom when the picture slowly emerges on the whitish paper. For me that's a moment of creation, of productivity. The transition from a white nothingness to a something as yet indistinct is fluid and surprises with its constantly changing structures. The slow coming-into-being of a form. A germination that I bring about, control; that I can interrupt. Conception. A chemistry of budding life, in which I'm involved. It was different with my children, my unborn children. I never had the feeling of being involved. Maybe it would have come later, much later. When something started to move inside me. As it was, all I had were the two interruptions.

The first child would have come too soon. Hinner and I were still in medical school and had other worries. The second I didn't want; I knew I wouldn't be staying with Hinner. Or rather, I sensed it, as one instinctively senses danger long before it arrives. We didn't belong together. Actually we never fought or had scenes; we simply didn't belong together. Why bring a child into all that? Hinner was upset when he got to the hospital. I hadn't told him anything beforehand, and perhaps he already suspected I would leave him. He didn't reproach me, he was just profoundly upset. I felt sorry for him, but that was no reason to have a child.

After each abortion I was physically exhausted, dead tired. Wanting only to rest.

I was in despair without being able to say why. A dull pain in the back of my head kept me from sleeping for more than a few hours at a time. It wasn't guilt. I hadn't felt any bond with the thing growing inside me, nothing to make me upset about losing it. Probably the despair came from my weakened physical condition. I had nothing to do with these children, I wasn't involved. It was just something that happened to me. I hadn't wanted them, they were there against my will. I felt used by him. An incubating vessel, the caretaker for his embryos. I hadn't wanted a child, yet he could make one start growing inside me. I wasn't consulted, I didn't count, I wasn't involved, I was just an object. While he whispered in my ear, moaned, repeated endearments, he was deciding for me, for my body, for my future. A monstrous intervention that would determine my entire life, an intervention in my freedom. I liked sleeping with him; we were good in bed, as they say. Sex wasn't the problem, even if later on Hinner—surprisingly—concluded that it had to be. When I said we should separate because there was nothing between us anymore, he immediately asked whether I was dissatisfied with him as a man. I tried to explain, but he didn't understand. Then he decided it was because of his tacky affairs with student nurses. In his eyes all our difficulties came down to the bedroom. His fear of failing as a man was so overwhelming that it made him deaf to our actual problems. His reaction was probably the typical masculine response. A product of hundreds of years of patriarchal society: the more power men wield, the less human they become. And since this power is based on gender as the primary differentiating and dominating factor, naturally those who wield it attach excessive importance to sex. In men's thoughts and fantasies, in their conversations and jokes, sex always comes first. Topic number one, burdensome, oppressive, overpowering. Liberation leading to denial, to impotence, a man's domain, room to play, a furlough from oppressive responsibility. Here the presence of women is unsuitable, a betrayal, a nuisance on nights out with the boys. But then there is also flirtation with precisely this betrayal, flirtation a man uses to stake out his room to play, his freedom, like a carefully guarded treasure that he speaks of proudly, lewdly, enthusiastically, or with restraint. This treasure has to remain hidden so it isn't lost;

a man has to speak of it though, to be admired as its owner. I couldn't interpret Hinner's reaction any other way. He was defending something he felt was threatened.

I think women take sex more lightly, less obsessively. More naturally, because their sex organs are also used for real work. Bearing children is work. That prevents glorified expectations as well as anxiety and fear. An attitude that disturbs men, because it displaces the norm, their norm, what they call normal. That's why they fight it, punish it. In order to preserve the rites of their faith, their concept of sexuality, and to assert it as the only valid one, they condemn as frigid the Other that doesn't bow to their wishes, that doesn't subordinate itself to them and their fantasies. A necessary ritual. An exorcism of anxiety. Prisoners in the world of their own concepts.

Hinner's attacks didn't bother me. And I didn't have the strength to pity him. I had nothing to do with his child. I conceived it as indifferently as it was removed from inside me. Someone else's property. I lay on a bed, a table, my legs strapped down, my pubic hair shaved, shaved off completely. Then an injection, an anesthetic, a slight pain from some liquid dripping on me. Then a haze, through which single, disconnected words swim into my consciousness. Futile attempts to reach me. I keep hearing my name spoken pleadingly, demandingly, anxiously. I've gone under, deep below my consciousness, below my self. I refuse to leave the fog I'm hiding in; it protects me. I'm afraid of falling out of its safety, of having to accept this body as my own, of seeing my legs forcibly spread apart, strapped down, with dark bruises from their restless thrashing. Between my legs their voices, the gentle clinking of instruments, and again his breathing, his whispering, his endearments. Behind my eyelids a huge, glaring sun, coming closer. I want to be alone, just alone. Leave me alone, I don't want to, I don't want to any more, I whisper. It's hard to speak. My tongue is like a stopper, choking me, making me gag. I find it impossible to conclude a thought, to conclude anything. Then the woods are there, a cool, overcast sky, the path that leads to a bridge, broken remains. I crawl into the grass, under the trees. I feel branches scratching me, the coolness of the earth, wet leaves.

No, the woman stretched out on the table wasn't me, isn't me. I had nothing to do with that.

The wet pictures are stuck together. I'm not unhappy with them. The more I work in the darkroom, the less I hope for unexpectedly perfect pictures, for an amazing sight captured by the instrument, something I didn't notice in the viewfinder. There's no amazement, no unexpected discovery. The camera reliably delivers what you ask of it, nothing more.

While I was drying the pictures, the doorbell rang. Frau Rupprecht, my neighbor, was standing there in a bathrobe. Her gray hair hung around her face, unkempt and stringy, surprisingly short. Usually she wears it in a bun, and I had assumed it came down to her shoulders.

She apologized for disturbing me so late. I looked at my watch: already past midnight. I said she wasn't disturbing me, I was still doing things. She asked me for pills. Her heart was acting up, she couldn't lie down without getting shooting pains.

I have this uneasiness, you know what I mean? she said.

She didn't look directly at me. Her eyes roamed around

the hall, anxious as the eyes of a dog that's just been beaten. I calmed her down and told her to leave her door open, I'd be right over.

As I was taking pills out of the bathroom cabinet, I realized how tired I was. I splashed cold water on my face, dried it, and went to her apartment.

She was sitting in her armchair. I gave her the pills and told her to stay put. I went into her kitchen, rinsed out a glass, and filled it with water. Her apartment was clean, but there was a pungent smell. It probably came from the birds. Frau Rupprecht has a lot of birds. She keeps them in several cages that hang on the wall like picture frames. When I brought her the water, she reached for my hand. She had this uneasiness inside her, she said, as if some disaster were coming. But she didn't have children anymore, only the birds. When I asked whether it wasn't too hard for her to take care of so many birds, she gazed at me blankly.

My birds are all I have left, she said.

She asked me to stay a moment. She was afraid of being alone. Then she talked about her husband and her son, both of whom were dead. Her husband died twelve years ago of a pulmonary embolism. The son had a fatal accident on his motorcycle; he would have been twenty-three now. Frau Rupprecht had already told me the story, but I listened without interrupting. Then she talked about her uneasiness. She always felt it before something bad happened. That's how it was before her son was killed and when her husband died. And before other disasters too. When she felt this uneasiness, things were bad. So now she knew that something awful was happening, somewhere in the world.

She held my hand and shut her eyes. I thought she'd gone to sleep. When I tried to leave, she began again. I didn't immediately realize that she was talking about her son.

I had no idea how much a child can hurt you, she said.

She told the story of the accident again. After a while I asked whether she was feeling better. She thanked me and apologized. I helped her get into bed, then went back to my apartment. I was hungry, but the kitchen was full of photography equipment. So I just drank some brandy and lay down.

The next day I got up late, since I wasn't on call until the afternoon. I rang Frau Rupprecht's bell. She was feeling well again, her eyes were clear. She said once more that she was sorry for bothering me, and I told her to stop apologizing. She asked me in for a cup of coffee, but I said I didn't have time. Then she told me about an airplane crash in Spain. She heard it on the radio: a passenger plane had gone down last night. Did I think that might have caused her uneasiness? I said I didn't know, but I didn't see how it could. She laughed at herself and said, I'm a crazy old woman, right?

I was relieved that she was feeling better, and told her so.

During the morning I dried the rest of the pictures and tidied up the kitchen and bathroom. Then I made myself some breakfast. In between I went down in the elevator to check the mail. Only newspapers and the telephone bill. Shortly before twelve I left for the hospital. As I drove I thought about what to do with the pictures. I wouldn't mind hanging them in my room for a while. But there were too many. Probably I'd end up packing them away somewhere, for some later time that would never come.

It was pointless to send them home. Mother would scrutinize each one to see if she could learn something about me. She's still hoping to have some part in my life.

I thought of Frau Rupprecht; I should look in on her more often. Her uneasiness obviously came from being alone too much.

There was no space in front of the hospital. I had to park the car on a side street.

8

. . . .

There were a lot of tourists in town now. But as soon as the stores closed, the streets emptied and looked as desolate as ever.

I often went walking with Henry in our park. And twice we went to the movies. Both times American films, full of high-speed chases. Cars kept falling off cliffs and exploding.

The air in the theater was suffocating. I had to go outside partway through the movie. Breathing in the smell of my sweaty neighbors gave me something like claustrophobia.

One Saturday morning I went shopping with Henry. We bought him a suit. It was a dark, double-breasted pinstripe, and he looked elegant in it. He bought it even though he said he'd never wear it. I was looking for some makeup and some nice earthenware dishes for everyday use, and Henry patiently tagged along.

At the hospital I had a lot to do. Since it was vacation time, I had other patients besides my own. Twice I had to take calls for colleagues, and when I got home I was too tired to do anything. On days like that I'm very pleased with my apartment. It's so small and well set up that I can just let things slide.

The hot weather was annoying, because the heat builds up in my room. In the evening I open all the doors and let the shower run for a long time, but it doesn't help much. So I have a hard time falling asleep, and the street noise wakes me early.

In September my mother phoned me at the hospital. She said Father wasn't well. When I asked whether I should come, she said that wasn't why she had called. I told her I could take a day off anytime, if Father was ill. It wasn't that bad, she said, not that bad. She just wanted to hear my voice. I promised to visit soon.

After the conversation I thought about driving out there with Henry. But I knew Mother, she'd make such a fuss over Henry and me that the visit would just be one big embarrassment.

That evening I wrote to Father. I tried to sound loving. I wanted to make it a long letter, but after half a page of fancy phrases I couldn't think of anything else to say. So I apologized for that. On the way to the post office, I tore it up. It seemed so phony. I would have liked to write him an affectionate letter, but once the empty page was in front of me I didn't know what to say. Maybe I'm just no good at letters. I decided to go out there soon.

The chief invited me to visit him and his wife again. After a staff meeting, he asked me to stay a moment. He had me sit back down and offered me a cigarette, then fidgeted and fiddled with his glasses. Thinking he was embarrassed because there had been some complaint about me, I smiled at him. Finally he said his wife would like it if I could stop by to see them. He said it very ironically, which I didn't understand. Maybe it was her wish, and he was just carrying out orders.

I thanked him, and he said that was all. Now we were both embarrassed. It was ridiculous; I didn't know whether I should go or stay. Then he bent over his desk, and I stood up.

Thank you very much for the invitation, I said.

He looked up for a second and said haughtily, Well, if you have the time, but I know . . .

He didn't complete the sentence.

As I returned to my office, I was thinking about him. I imagine he feels old and lonely. He's afraid of being rejected, so he buries himself in his work and his solitude. But I wasn't sure. I didn't understand him. And I had no desire to get to know him better. Why should I concern myself with his problems, traumas, fears? I'm not interested in the various miseries and destinies of this person or that. I already have too much to worry about with myself, with my work. I can prescribe pills and give injections. The rest isn't the responsibility of medicine. I'm not a priest, I don't dole out consolation. I consider it presumptuous and dishonest to tell anyone to cheer up. I have my own problems, and even they interest me only to a degree, and not very often. Essentially only when I'm out of control, when I let myself go. When I succumb to emotion. Real problems can't be solved anyway; you drag them around with you all your life; they are life, and at some point you die of them. My grandparents' generation had folk sayings like: Fear will disappear if you look it in the eye. My experience has been different. The thing you fear most can do you in, so why focus on it? And you certainly can't help other people. That's not cynical really, just the opposite. If I experiment around with a terminally ill patient, I degrade him into a laboratory animal. He'll die without me, too, but more easily, with less effort. And he'll waste less energy on empty hopes. I know it's become customary in our century to diagnose inhibitions, to expose them, to hoist them to the level of consciousness. They are considered symptoms, and treated as such. Now it's common knowledge that everybody has a wounded psyche, a disturbed relationship to himself, to his own little world. So everybody's sick in one way or another. A new fad: illness caused by medicine, the fatal science. What good does it do to make people aware of their inhibitions? Repression is self-defense, defense against danger. Designed to help the organism exist. A living being tries to survive by not perceiving various things that could destroy it. A healthy natural mechanism. Why exhume these corpses that no one can live with anyway? In the final analysis, all of civilization is one big repression. Human beings discovered they could live in society provided they repressed certain feelings and drives. Not until the species as a whole had reached a state where it needed psychiatrists was it capable of living as a society. Repression produced what we call civilized man.

To live in society at all, individuals apparently have to set up barriers inside themselves. The deep, dark dungeons of our souls, where we incarcerate anything that threatens the thin layer of our humanity. Every day I repress a flood of events and feelings that hurt and humiliate me. Otherwise I wouldn't be able to get out of bed in the morning. Barriers that separate us from chaos. A slight tear in our tender skin lets the blood gush out. At the sight of an open, beating heart, most people get sick to their stomachs. A simple hollow muscle that functions pretty much mechanically takes their breath away, causes them to sweat, vomit, faint. Yet this little bundle of flesh and blood has such an important place in our consciousness that it serves as a symbol of our most beautiful feelings. Of course, that's when it's discreetly hidden beneath a more human-seeming surface, covered over with smooth layers of fat and a soft epidermis. Think how terrified we'd be if we had to look at all the layers of sediment at the bottom of our existence. And why dredge up things that trouble us, threaten us, make us helpless? Our personal radioactive waste, which remains potent indefinitely, whose almost inaudible rumblings alarm us, and with which we can live only if we entomb it, seal it, and sink it in our deepest depths. In inaccessible oblivion.

We've settled on the surface. A limit imposed by both reason and civilization.

A woman colleague described the case of a psyche gone astray in the thicket of its inner world. The man was thirty-four and the head of a relatively stable household, with a well-balanced sexual economy. His interest in psycho-sociological literature introduced him to the phenomena of sexual disturbance, which he eventually diagnosed in himself. This intense preoccupation with himself, the relentless exploration and recording of every twitch and quiver of his psyche, finally produced in him a full-blown castration anxiety. All the more incurable because he had read all the pertinent literature and blocked his therapy with his home-grown self-diagnosis. Hospital humor.

Another favorite: At the university hospital a colleague responds to an impotent man's cry for help: My God, be glad you're rid of it!

Medical wit. I don't find it so funny anymore. Another result of our psycho-diagnosis: if you analyze a joke thoroughly, it stops being funny.

Anyway, none of this is very important. My lack of interest in it is the most effective protection.

Carla told me Henry had called and she had said I was on night duty. He would call again later.

Henry had been in Prague for a week. A business trip: he was supposed to look over the reconstruction work being done on some historic building, a theater, I think. He had promised to call from Prague, but he didn't.

That night he showed up around ten o'clock. I was sitting in the doctors' lounge next to the emergency room. A colleague from gynecology had stopped by to see me, and we were discussing salaries. He and his wife had separate bank accounts, he said. Sometimes they lent each other money, but each saw to it that the other paid up on schedule. Finances are taboo, sacred and untouchable, the true intimate realm. Mutual use of the sexual organs may be the original, archaic form of marriage; the civilized cohabitation of two human beings follows more refined patterns.

When Henry came in, my colleague stood up. I introduced them. Neither said anything. They appraised each other in silence, with guarded smiles and searching looks at me. A couple of years ago I would have tried to say something, make some banal remark to relieve the silence. I used to chatter stupidly, say things I was ashamed of afterward. Anything to avoid the pressure of gaps in the conversation. That's over now; I broke myself of it. I've trained myself not to escape from uncomfortable situations by spouting trivia. Now I enjoy the nervous, crackling silence, the embarrassment that spreads palpably, the tension that grows like an avalanche. The longing for an end to the unexpected pause, which becomes all the more difficult to end the longer it lasts.

Henry stared at the glass case, my colleague cleared his throat. He was still standing. Then he said something about getting back to his patients and not wanting to disturb us. He winked at me in relief and left the room. Henry asked who he was. Without waiting for an answer, he said he didn't like him. I didn't respond.

Then Henry talked about Prague. He apologized for not phoning. At his hotel you couldn't make long-distance calls, and they told him at the post office he'd have to wait at least two hours. He asked whether I understood that he couldn't sit around a Prague post office for two hours. He had come to me directly from the airport. I offered to send out for food or coffee, but he didn't want anything.

Until 11:30 it was quiet on the wards. The nurse called me twice, but she took care of everything else herself. She didn't want to disturb me.

I lay on the cot, and Henry sat beside me and talked. I listened more to his voice than to what he was saying. Later he pulled his chair closer and fumbled with the buttons on my blouse. I told him to stop. He didn't understand why we shouldn't sleep together there. He was annoyed. I said he couldn't sit with me all night, he should go home. But he stayed. He didn't have to go to work the next day.

It was pleasant to know he was there next to me. I felt relaxed and protected. The noises from outside hardly penetrated, and once I even fell asleep for a few minutes. Henry didn't notice, or at least he didn't mention it.

Shortly after midnight I was called out to see a married couple. The wife was suffering from nervous heart palpitations. For days she'd been having to sleep sitting up. I talked with both of them, did an electrocardiogram, and gave her a tranquilizer. I said that most cases of this sort didn't have an organic cause but resulted from a troubled relationship with the outside world. I asked about her work and her marriage. The woman bridled at what she called my insinuations. She had no trouble at work, she said, everyone thought well of her. And there was nothing wrong with her marriage; she certainly had no need to get her husband's attention through imaginary illnesses. I tried to explain that her heart problems weren't imaginary in my view, but that they were probably the result of psychic disturbances. She blushed furiously: You seem to think I need a psychiatrist. No, I said.

I gave her some pills that wouldn't help her but wouldn't do her any harm. She said she was going to see another doctor, and I encouraged her to do so. She had no confidence in me, so there was no point in her coming back. She left the room without saying good-bye. Her husband was tired. He didn't seem to understand much of what had happened.

If you're right, he finally said, it would be bad. Then no doctor can help her.

I nodded. We could hear his wife's shrill voice calling him from outside. I'm coming, he said, and got up. He stood there and looked at me thoughtfully.

If your wife wants to get better, I said, she'll have to help herself. Maybe you'll have to change some things in your marriage; all we can do is offer support.

I don't know if she'll be able to find the courage, he said. She called him again. He shook my hand and thanked me before he left.

In the meantime our "night shelter" had begun to fill up. The corridor of the emergency room was crowded with the drunk and injured. Some were waiting to be treated, others to be driven home. In the two examining rooms lay three drunks, helpless and splattered with blood. Now and then one of them would get noisy and an orderly or a nurse would start shouting at them. After being examined and treated, drunks are released or sent to the lockup.

At 12:30 three men were brought in for blood tests; the police had stopped them on the road. One of them kept threatening us, saying we'd be hearing from him. Another was agitated and breathing hard through his mouth. When I asked him to roll up his sleeve, he whispered that he'd give me five hundred marks if I helped him out. To be precise, he said: If you can work something out for me. I told him loudly to shut up. He looked across at the policeman, who was watching us without interest. Then he fell silent, but he threw me a look full of hatred as he left.

I sent Henry away. You ought to go home, I said. I didn't want him to spend the whole night here. I had work to do now. We kissed, and I promised to phone and wake him in the morning.

I didn't like him to watch me at work. It distracted and

disturbed me. Because he was curious, I had let him spend a night with me two weeks before. I was on ambulance duty. I was under no obligation; in our wards we were on call at night often enough. But an acquaintance had asked me to substitute for him, and I'd said yes.

That night we had to cover a dance. The dispatcher had already sent one medical team and now ordered our ambulance to the scene.

The dance was in a factory cafeteria. The guard opened the gate when we honked. We drove into the courtyard and parked next to the other ambulance. Music was blaring from the open windows on the second floor. Several young people leaning on the windowsills watched us drive in. They called down to us, but the music drowned them out.

The coat-check area had been set up on the ground floor. That was where the injured were sitting. A doctor from the other ambulance was examining them while two policemen and several young men were standing around. The injured seemed apathetic. They were a little drunk and stared listlessly ahead. Most of them had superficial lacerations that were already scabbing over, so it was too late to stitch them up. I greeted my colleague and asked what needed to be done. The driver put two young men into the ambulance and drove them off to the hospital. One seemed to have a broken nose. It would need to be X-rayed. The other apparently had two broken fingers. The rest of the injured were patched up with gauze and adhesive tape. There wasn't much work; a second ambulance hadn't been necessary. The young men who were standing around pulled the injured up from their chairs and escorted them roughly to the factory gate.

Henry wanted to see the dance. We went up the broad, winding staircase. On the left was a refreshment stand, with a sour smell of spilled beer and hot sausage. The vendor, a bald man of fifty, was wearing shorts and a stained smock, open over his bare chest.

On the other side three large doors led into the makeshift ballroom. We looked in the first door and saw a stage lit by colored strobe lights. The room was dark. The music was ear-shattering, painful. Young people sat at long tables with bottles of schnapps in front of them. Between the rows, figures staggered about, leaning on the shoulders of those who were seated. Three couples were dancing, holding each other close. The large speakers were pointed in their direction; it must have been unbearable.

When my eyes adjusted to the dim light, I saw that only girls were dancing. Girls were also sitting by themselves at the tables. None of the boys showed any interest in them, they just guzzled schnapps dully. At one table four men were growling something like a song, but the music from the loudspeakers drowned them out and they soon gave up.

When the musicians took a break and left the stage, we heard a babble of voices, shouts, a girl squealing. Then the music came flooding out again, this time on tape.

We went out. I felt my right temple beginning to throb.

In the lobby one of the musicians was standing with the singer, a woman wearing a glittery dress and too much makeup. Completely surrounded by young people in jeans, she looked somehow lost and rare, like an exotic butterfly.

Do you like our music? she asked me.

I can't tell, I said, it's so loud.

It's crap, she agreed, but that's what they want.

Why isn't anyone dancing? Henry asked.

Don't know, they never dance. They just come, the singer remarked indifferently.

And what are they looking for? Henry continued.

Don't know. Some shit or other, she answered, smiling. She offered us red wine, which she was drinking out of the bottle.

I explained that we were on duty, and she smiled.

The young men who had hustled out the injured came up the stairs. One of them, who was maybe eighteen, approached us.

Any problems? he asked, and immediately answered himself: Everything's under control.

He gave us a self-satisfied wink and went into the ballroom with his friends. We watched them pass through the rows, here and there giving someone a shove. A man had slumped down under the table; they pulled him to his feet and took him out. At the stairs they gave him a shove. The drunk staggered down the steps without falling and landed in front of the coat-check counter. The two who had pushed him laughed and came over to us. The young man winked again and said: We run a tight ship here.

They went back into the hall.

The order patrol, the musician explained to us. Without them this place would be a lot wilder.

I could easily imagine that.

This isn't exactly my scene, the singer declared.

What would you like to do? I asked.

Don't know. Something different. The shitty part is, you don't meet anyone interesting here. They all get sloshed, and my boys only care about lining up something to go to bed with afterwards.

The musician protested.

You know it's true, she interrupted him; Who do you think comes here?

She must have been about my age. All the makeup made her look older.

You can't ever have a real conversation, you know, she said to me.

We went down the stairs. The two policemen were standing by our ambulance talking to the driver.

Henry asked them, What are those kids up there waiting for? They come here and then sit around waiting?

Hell, one of the policemen said, they just want to booze it up.

Booze it up and cause trouble, the other agreed.

They both laughed.

No, Henry said, they're waiting for something to happen. They're hoping something will happen. Anything, maybe their lives.

The policemen looked at each other. Their silence spoke volumes. As we were getting into the ambulance, one of them asked Henry: Are you a doctor?

Yes, I replied, and Henry said simultaneously: No.

What then? the policeman asked.

He's my husband, I said.

The policeman nodded. Then he turned to me and said, Your husband's not allowed to ride in the ambulance. You know that.

No one answered. We drove off.

Henry spent the rest of that night with me in the doctors' lounge. We had to make two more runs, and both times he came along. I think he was somehow disappointed. My work isn't very exciting.

In any case, after that night I didn't want him around again when I was on call. So now I asked him to go. I stood in front of the hospital and watched his car drive off. It was cold, I was shivering. The sky was cloudless, indifferently presenting the glory of its stars. The blood was pounding in my head. That was from exhaustion. I took a deep breath. Then I went back into the building.

9

. . . .

In the middle of October I drove to G. I had two days off, and I didn't want to spend them in Berlin.

The trip was a surprise even to me. A day beforehand, on Wednesday, I called up the only hotel in G. and was still able to book a room for one night.

Why I wanted to go there I can't say. I spent my childhood in G. When I was fourteen my parents moved, and I'd never been back.

I called Henry at work and told him I was taking a two-day vacation. He asked if he could come along. I said it would be something like a trip into the past for me, and he'd be bored. Two hours later I called again and said I'd be happy if he would come. He laughed and asked if I was afraid of waking the ghosts of the past, or had something else changed my mind? I said I hadn't thought anything through and really didn't have a good reason for going to G. And if I was afraid of anything, it was of being bored to death for two days in a backwater that I had no connection with. Henry advised me to go to any town except G. He said it wouldn't help me, it was an ill-considered trip back to a past long gone. I said I just wanted to take a look, check my memories, no more. We agreed to meet for breakfast.

The next morning we set out around nine o'clock. We took Henry's car. On the way he asked me to tell him something about G., and about my childhood. I described the town, our house. I talked about my parents and my sister, about the school, the small classroom, my friendships, passions, innumerable secrets.

We laughed a lot during the drive. The sudden notion of visiting my hometown no longer struck me as odd or requiring explanation.

When we arrived and drove through G., I felt a mounting tension. To distract myself I talked a lot. I told Henry how to get to the hotel, but since I had only vague recollections, it was some time before we reached the Golden Anchor.

We had to wait at the desk until a girl appeared from

the kitchen. She was fat and suspicious and answered in monosyllables. We managed to get a room for Henry; no doubles were available.

While we were filling out the registration form, the girl stared at us. Then she gave us the keys and pointed to a sign listing the restaurant hours. She read through our registrations. Finally she reached for a thick book and copied in our names and addresses.

I was already on the stairs when it occurred to me to ask her about the other guests. She didn't understand me, and I had to explain why I was asking. Then she said, They're people traveling on business and so on. People like yourself.

I asked her to let me look at the guest book. She stared in amazement, snapped the book shut without a word, and stuck it into a drawer. She put both hands on the counter, two red, chafed hands, which definitely barricaded the book, and gazed at me blankly. She wouldn't disappear into her kitchen until I'd gone to my room.

Henry asked what I wanted from her. I laughed and said I had suddenly wondered who besides us had any reason to come to G. and spend the night in this hole. And then I had imagined a gathering of my old schoolmates. Otherwise I couldn't think of one reason for anyone to travel here. For a moment I'd felt sure that all the rooms in the Golden Anchor were taken by my old school friends who, like me, had come back because they wanted to explore their memories for a few days.

I know it was stupid, I said, but it would be funny.

In the afternoon we walked through the town. Everything was small, much smaller than I remembered. Still, it seemed unchanged. Even the ancient, faded sign above the grocery store across from my old school was holding its own against the weather and the march of history: Colonial Wares, Southern Fruits, Imports.

I went through the town as if I were wearing a magic cap that made me invisible: I saw, I recognized, and no one recognized me. I hadn't been in G. for over twenty-five years. Nothing seemed changed, even though I knew that everything was different, had to be different. But I wouldn't notice that. For me G. would remain the home of a twelve-year-old girl, filled with her hopes and fears. I felt connected with that girl, but in a strange, distant way.

Since we weren't very hungry at lunchtime, I bought some pastry at a bakery in the marketplace. A young blonde woman behind the counter asked in a friendly voice what I wanted. New shelves had been put up, but the walls were still tiled like a butcher shop's. To the right a door led into the kitchen. It was open, as it always had been. Behind the second door, with its glass pane and white curtains, were the living quarters of the baker, Wirsing. In my time Frau Wirsing would occasionally peer through the curtain into the bakery. If a line was forming or she saw an acquaintance in the shop, she would come out and serve people herself.

The blonde salesgirl wrapped up my pastries with quick, practiced movements. I asked if the baker's wife was home and if I could speak to her.

Just a moment, she said, and rapped on the curtained window. The door opened, and the salesgirl said something I couldn't hear. Then a stout woman of about fifty appeared at the door. Her hair was dyed dark red, with one silver curl. She was wearing an apron. As she came toward me, she pursed her lips inquiringly.

What can I do for you? she asked.

I didn't reply. She stood there before me, her lips still pursed.

Can I help you? she asked.

I shook my head. Please excuse me, I thought you were someone else.

I paid, took the packet of pastry, and we went out. The new owner and her salesgirl looked after us.

Don't do that again, Henry said gently, when we were standing outside.

In the old days, I said, we used to get pie crusts from Frau Wirsing. For ten pfennigs she would give us a huge bag full. We came by every afternoon and stuffed ourselves.

Henry nodded, to placate me.

We walked all over town until evening. We went to Miller's Hill and to the old mill. I showed him G.'s two tourist attractions: Queen Luise's Rock and the Schiller Room. We also visited Bismarck Gardens just outside of town, a spacious park with a fountain and a small zoo. Now they had deer, a mountain goat, and parrots. The cage that used to hold a snowy owl was empty. I was amazed at how few animals there were. I remembered brown bears, donkeys, wolves. I must have been mistaken, there wasn't enough room. They couldn't ever have been there, not even in my childhood.

Henry liked the gardens. Wouldn't I enjoy working there as a gardener or a zookeeper? he asked.

Back in town, in front of the stationery store, a woman holding a child by the hand was walking toward us. I recognized her instantly: It was Lucie Brehm. I wanted to speak to her. Henry realized what I had in mind and reached for my hand. Forget it, he said softly and firmly. He was right; he was the more sensible of us two. It had been a thoughtless impulse on my part.

Lucie Brehm, or whatever her name was now, must have noticed my interest. She looked at me, and I smiled at her. Her expression did not change. She had become prettier. Her stupid, plump child's face had taken on gentle lines. Her eyes still had a helpless look to them, but what had seemed false and obsequious to us then now had something of a perceptive glow.

Maybe my smile surprised her. She looked at me thoughtfully. Then she turned her eyes away and walked past, pulling the child behind her.

I told Henry about her. Lucie sat two rows in front of me. No one liked her, for no particular reason. She kept trying to make friends with one or another of the girls in our class. It didn't work, she simply wasn't accepted. Something about her bothered us, I don't know what now, and I didn't know then. It was an unwritten law in the class that no one should make friends with Lucie Brehm. I would never have dared to go against that, and I'm sure I didn't want to, either. She was the only one of us who didn't own a gym uniform. She came to gym in her pink panties. Once when she was hanging from the pull-up bar, some girl reached up and, quick as lightning, pulled off her panties. Lucie fell onto the mat in shock and embarrassment. We thought it was hilarious, and even the gym teacher laughed. We found it comical the way she tried to retrieve her panties, which were only a few steps away from the mat. Lucie didn't want to stand up and expose herself entirely, so with one hand over her thighs, which she pressed together, she tried to reach for the panties. Not one of us helped her. Herr

Ebert, the gym teacher, came over and picked up the panties with his thumb and forefinger. He dangled them over Lucie's head. She tried to reach them but couldn't without standing up. Finally he dropped them, and Lucie quickly pulled them on. She didn't cry at all, which surprised me. She wasn't even mad. She looked at us, ashamed and humble, still begging for our affection. The word was that she was a goody-goody; no one wanted anything to do with her.

We were all afraid of Herr Ebert. Even the star athletes. They were his pets, and he was merciless when they let him down. His favorite epithets were "Rotten Cherry" and "Flabby Squirt," terms he would drawl out slowly, voluptuously, while the poor victim dangled from the pull-up bar or between the rungs of the parallel bars. The rest of us laughed. The closer our turn came to perform, the louder and more enthusiastically we would laugh. The imminent danger of his ridicule made us so tense we couldn't do the simplest exercise. Fear weighed us down like lead even before our sweaty palms took hold of the bars, poles, and ropes. Herr Ebert's remarks dripped down on us like a sticky mass that made us immobile, rigid and lifeless. We didn't realize—I didn't realize—until much later that his name-calling was aimed at wounding us in more than just our athletic pride. Only girls were "Rotten Cherries," only boys were "Flabby Squirts."

I no longer know the name of the gym teacher in the upper school. In my memory it's Herr Ebert, but it had to be a different teacher, because it was a different school in a different town. Everything was different, yet little changed. The new Herr Ebert liked having the exercises demonstrated. He would pick the three or four prettiest and most developed girls and have them constantly performing flips on the bars or doing gymnastics. Blushing furiously, the girls demonstrated the exercises again and again under the teacher's lascivious gaze, while the remainder of the class, to which I fortunately belonged, the late bloomers, giggled quietly as we observed the teacher's game. We felt sorry for those girls and envied them at the same time. I spent whole gym classes sitting on the bench watching the new Herr Ebert benevolently lecture his chosen ones, persuading them over and over again to leap and gyrate in front of him. He was generous in his willingness to act as spotter, which officially sanctioned his touching the girls' bodies.

For years after I got out of school I felt clumsy, unathletic: like a "Rotten Cherry." And when I finally reached the point where I could talk about it, other people spoke, hesitantly and cautiously, of similar experiences. Everyone had had his Herr Ebert, everyone could still feel, years later, the firm, painful grip, the caustic remarks. I think my generation went down on their gym mat so hard that we still feel it in every organ (also in our rotten cherries and flabby squirts). Somehow this physical fitness training debilitated us for good.

Of course this is all exaggerated, subjective, untenable. A distorted private impression, without adequate understanding of the actual problems, difficulties, and successes. Obviously I lack the overview to evaluate the experiences properly. I lack the overview because I'm still down on the mat.

Henry had listened to me attentively. With a smile he said again, Forget it.

In the evening we decided to go to the movies so we wouldn't have to sit in the hotel dining room or in our rooms. We ate beforehand at the Black Lion, a tavern. All they had was goulash soup, and we each ordered a large bowl and a basket of bread. We were hungry, and no other restaurants were open. The soup tasted watery; we ate a lot of bread. The locals, men my age or older, sat drinking their beer and observing us in silence. I didn't recognize any of them.

At the movie theater we had to wait. The cashier explained that they would show the picture only if five people turned up. Two teenage boys were standing outside. Henry and I stayed in the lobby and smoked.

At five past eight the boys came in with two girls and asked for tickets. The cashier reached grumpily for the roll of tickets. One of the girls said she didn't want to go to the movies, and ran outside. Her friend followed her. Then one of the boys ran after them and came back with both of them. He had wound one girl's hair around his finger and was dragging her behind him. He let her go in front of the booth. Now the girls wanted to see the movie, but they demanded that the boys pay for them. The boys refused. The cashier shouted at them, and the girls finally pulled out their money.

The theater hadn't changed. The same rows of folding seats with the ripped red upholstery, the shiny olive-green paint on the walls.

The light was on, but the projectionist had already started the film while we were standing at the ticket booth. It was a Spanish movie about a worker who is fired from his job and moves his family to a village. There were beautiful shots of landscapes. We were bored and left. The teenagers weren't watching any more, either; they were busy necking.

The door to the outside was locked. We had to get the

cashier to let us out, which she did with a hostile look. If we hadn't come, she would have had the evening off.

The hotel was locked too. When we rang the night bell, a crippled doorman came to open up and give us our room keys. It was only nine, but I wanted to sleep and said good night to Henry.

An hour later, I got up, put on my clothes, and went downstairs to the doorman. I asked him if he could sell me a bottle of wine, but he said it was impossible at this hour. So I gave him ten marks, and he got me three bottles of beer from the refrigerator. Back in my room I sat in the one chair and smoked. I wouldn't be able to fall asleep for the next two or three hours. I knew myself; there was no sense in even trying.

The trip to G. was pointless, and I regretted having come with Henry. Embarrassment you bring on yourself is easier to bear alone. The past can't be recovered. Nothing remains in us but vague fragments and notions, distorted, prettied up, wrong. Nothing can be verified. My memories have become irrefutable facts. The past is the way I've preserved it, the way I retain it. My dreams can't be spoiled any more, my fears can't be extinguished. My G. no longer exists. This town forgot the earlier town a long time ago, and completely. The testimony in brick and stone may give an illusion of similarity, but the rain has washed that time away once and for all. There is no returning, no homecoming. Behind us are only burning cities, and she who looks back turns to a pillar of salt.

My old school had become a warehouse. Across from it was a modern structure, flat-roofed with large windows. The new school. In the afternoon I'd tried to look into my old classrooms, but the windowpanes on the first floor were blind, and all I could see was a vague reflection of my face. Henry had pressed me to move on. The windows in the upper story had been boarded up. The wall had been knocked out in the classroom where I and twenty-one other children had competed for the love of omnipotent teachers to shield us from the terror we felt at our own helplessness and dependency. A block and tackle hung from one of the beams of the old wall. This was where Herr Gerschke, the history teacher, had taught us.

I think all the girls were in love with Herr Gerschke. He always wore a suit and tie, even in the middle of summer. He was fair, and that was the highest praise we could give a teacher. I studied only for him. It was for him that I read extra books that bored me, in the hope of being praised by him. When we were in the sixth grade, he suddenly disappeared. There was much excitement at school and in town. People said he'd laid hands on a girl in the ninth grade. I was horrified. I imagined Herr Gerschke beating the girl, hitting her. I couldn't picture anything else that would fit the words "laid hands on," and the idea was unbearable. When I talked about it with another girl in my class, she said I was a dummy, Herr Gerschke had certainly not beaten the girl; on the contrary. I didn't understand, and she said he'd had an affair with the girl. Oh, I said, and acted as though I understood. Something like jealousy toward this girl in the ninth grade welled up in me, a kind of jealousy that was more a longing to be old enough to have Herr Gerschke notice me. See me for myself, not just praise me for the extra books I had read and my eagerness in class.

To be sure, I didn't understand why it was so bad that he'd had an affair with a student. When I said this to my mother, she decided to enlighten me. Alarmed by the goings-on at school, she did it with a vengeance. Along with my illusions she destroyed my loveliest dream, the hope of growing up quickly. I didn't want to marry any more, or at least, I wanted to marry very late. I knew now you absolutely had to avoid getting involved with a man too soon, that it took years to be sure of his love, that every woman was allowed to love only one single man, for whom she had to save herself. Terrible diseases, wasted figures covered with scabs and pus, a life whose only desire was death—these were the stern, insistent ghosts that pursued me for years. I was sixteen before I let a boy kiss me. And I rushed home afterwards to scrub myself from head to foot.

Years later, when I was already in medical school, I met my younger sister's boyfriend during a weekend at home. She was sixteen and he was in his early forties. He had graying temples and on his finger, the pale mark of the wedding ring he had slipped off. I watched my parents in amazement while they received him cordially and easily as their daughter's boyfriend. He who was scarcely younger than they. All their fears and anxieties had evaporated, having been transferred to me. They were free of anxiety, while I had to live with it. For years my mind was gummed up with distorted images of sexuality.

No one ever saw Herr Gerschke or the girl from the ninth grade again. The girl had moved away with her parents, and rumor had it that Herr Gerschke was in jail. Later we learned that he was teaching in another town. He'd been rehabilitated. His crime had been the product of that girl's imagination, her wishful thinking.

At the time he disappeared, we sensed the teachers' agitation, their nervousness. And we realized that in our powerlessness we had other ways of protecting ourselves besides docility, that salvation did not only lie in willing and complete subordination, that the omnipotent teachers were also in danger. In danger from us.

For two years our main teacher was Fräulein Nitschke, an older single woman. A Fräulein. Gaunt and sickly, her face heavily powdered, she sat behind the teacher's desk and read us prose and poetry. She tried to introduce us to the beauties of language, but we had been trained to listen or feign interest only in response to threats of punishment. She proved incapable of that game, and we made her suffer for it. She was obviously wounded when a stupid remark, an idiotic joke was our only reaction to one of the romantic poems she recited. She didn't punish us; she let us see that our stupidity and lack of understanding pained her. She must have wanted to educate us by not concealing the humiliation she suffered at our hands. She hoped that her dismay would shame us. We never forgave her for that.

Only once did we feel something like understanding for this woman who was so strange to us. On the day when the tanks came and we rushed to the window, she sat at her desk trembling uncontrollably. She seemed paralyzed. We gathered around and tried to soothe her. She didn't respond to anything we said. We were frightened, and two of the girls began crying hysterically. After a few minutes she calmed down. She was sweating and seemed exhausted. We offered to take her home, but she didn't want to leave the class without a teacher on a day like this. Not until the substitute arrived did she let two of the boys walk her to her lodgings. Later some people said she had been buried under rubble during the war. Others said she'd lived through the bombing of Dresden, in which her family was burned to death. She herself never said. For a few days we were chastened and obliging. But we soon forgot, and—at the mercy of the overweening authority of our teachers—we took revenge on that one teacher for all the violence perpetrated against us. On the only teacher who'd been willing to accept us as complicated little beings in our own right.

On the day of the tanks, the boys jumped up in the middle of class and ran to the window, shouting, The tanks are coming, the tanks are coming.

We heard the grinding, clanking sound of the tank tracks. Then it became quiet.

After school no one went home. We all knew that our parents wouldn't let us go out again, although curfew wasn't until evening. We ran to the marketplace. Only a single tank had come to G. It was parked in the middle of the square. The gun, covered with a tarpaulin, was pointed toward the weathered old First World War monument, which we were seeing for the first time. The day before, unknown persons had torn down the wooden structure with the large plywood peace dove and the decorative flag arrangement, and exposed the old monument underneath.

We stood with the crowd on the sidewalk and looked at the tank. Nothing was happening. People whispered to one another. Later the tank's upper hatch opened and a young Russian soldier looked out. He didn't seem to be afraid. He nodded to us. Then he climbed out. A policeman went up to him. The soldier said something and gestured, then kicked the tank's track with his boot. The policeman nodded and also gestured, explaining something with his hands. Then he too kicked the track. Both of them crouched and looked underneath the tank. Apparently the soldier was explaining something. Then he climbed back inside. The hatch closed. Things remained quiet, and I was getting bored. We went home.

The tank stayed only three days, and disappeared as suddenly as it had come. The boys said it had fired a shot during the night which had smashed through the walls of four houses, but the grown-ups said that was nonsense. The only thing that had been destroyed was the wooden structure with the plywood dove and the flags.

My father told us that they had come for the shoemaker's wife. She had provided the ax the unknown men had used to smash the peace monument. The shoemaker, her husband, was also taken to the regional capital, but he was back in G. two days later.

In the factory where Father worked as a foreman, everything remained quiet. Nevertheless he was agitated and kept screaming at my mother. I didn't understand any of it. Father told me I shouldn't ask questions in school or talk about what had happened. This wasn't the time. But in class nothing was said anyway. The children didn't ask and the teachers didn't explain. I didn't understand why, but since none of the grown-ups mentioned the tank, I sensed that even a conversation could be dangerous. I felt their fear of talking to each other. And I kept quiet so they wouldn't have to speak. I was afraid that if I forced them into a painful, reluctant discussion of one of their taboos, I would again be followed, all the way into my dreams, by wasted, disgusting people with venereal diseases. I learned to keep quiet.

I did talk about it with Katharina, my best friend, on our long walks to and from school. We had no secrets from each other. She was the daughter of an electrician who was killed in the war. She lived in a small house near the mill dam with her mother and three older brothers. The mother and two of the brothers worked in the same factory my father did. G. had only one factory then.

Katharina and I saw each other every day, even after school. After doing my homework I would go over to her house to pick her up. Hand in hand we would walk around town for hours; we went to the movies; we sat in her room. Still we never had enough time to talk.

Occasionally her older brothers also talked to me. They spoke somewhat superciliously to their little sister's friend, but they were always polite and willing to help us. I think I was in love with all three brothers. I wanted to be with them just as much as I suffered in their presence, from a terrible embarrassment which made me awkward and monosyllabic. I envied Katharina tremendously for her brothers.

Katharina and her family were religious. We had endless conversations about that too. I was enthralled by the fantastic stories in the Bible, by the strangely beautiful language, which I couldn't resist, and by this curious religious culture, both comical and awe-inspiring. Katharina took me to her Bible class, and since I knew the miracles and the passion of Christ by heart, the teacher would often give me colorful little picture cards illustrating some Biblical story.

Katharina and I had made a pact that we would always wear our hair the same way, also that we would come to a joint decision on the question of whether there was a God, or whether religion was in fact an invention meant to deceive the people, as we were taught in school. In the summer after our fourteenth birthdays we would decide together on an answer, and then be even more closely linked, either believing in God or rejecting him. We were both afraid of what our families would say when at last one or the other of us committed herself to a radically different world view, but aside from that we didn't see any difficulties. Religion attracted me very much, and I was becoming used to the idea that it would be I who gave my parents a big surprise.

My father wasn't happy that I was going to a Bible class, but after discussing it with my mother he decided to put up with it as a girl's adolescent emotionalism.

A year and a half before that summer of decision, he urged me to give up anything that had to do with the church or religion. He also asked me to think about my friendship with Katharina, since he was worried about my future. I didn't understand what he meant, but I did realize that he was concerned and wanted to help. Nevertheless, I refused to see my friend less often or to betray her in any way.

I heard from Katharina that Paul, her eldest brother, was no longer allowed to work as a brigade leader at the factory because he belonged to a Christian youth group. For the same reason the apprenticeship contract of her second brother, Frieder, had been changed so that he couldn't work in the trade he wanted. The brothers informed me that a campaign against religion was underway in the whole district. They were bitter, particularly because the factory management was dredging up ridiculous reasons to justify sanctions against them and other believers that lacked any and all legal basis. Katharina cried, and I felt guilty because I came from a family of athiests.

A few months later, after the third brother had finished school, all three of them disappeared. At first Katharina couldn't or wasn't allowed to tell me anything. Then I heard they had gone to West Germany, and she confirmed it. The brothers had leased a farm in Lower Saxony and were running it together.

Now my parents pressed me more often to break off my friendship with Katharina. In school too, well-meaning teachers indirectly or very directly pointed out that this friendship was not helping me.

That year the school board was to select the students in our class who would attend the university preparatory school in the district capital. Katharina and I both hoped to be chosen; for years we'd been the best in the class.

The decision came in October: a boy and I were selected. Our teacher announced that Katharina would have to leave school after finishing eighth grade, that in the opinion of the district authorities and the school board, she could not attain the educational goals of a secondary school in our Republic.

We both cried a good deal those days, and her mother was constantly having to comfort us. It was she who made me abandon my decision to give up secondary school in sympathy with Katharina. I was determined not to give in when my parents and teachers pressed me to end our friendship. In tears we swore to remain faithful to each other forever. Yet half a year later we were savage enemies.

Katharina had become friends with the son of the cantor. Though he was off in Naumburg studying sacred music, he spent weekends in G. and Katharina had less time for me. In spite of her detailed accounts of their meetings, I felt that something had come between us. Suspicion and jealousy crept into my love for Katharina. The pressures from teachers and parents, the school board's decision, the growing bitterness of Katharina's mother, who saw her daughter unjustly treated and now began to agree with and defend her sons' decision to leave the country and seek their fortune in the West—all this hovered unspoken between us. More and more often our conversations ended in a quarrel. Sometimes days went by before we saw each other again. Our mutual distrust grew; so did our mutual reserve, which drove a wedge between us even though we only meant to avoid hurting each other. At last all it took was a classmate's malicious remark to put an end to our friendship. A girl lied to Katharina about me behind my back, and Katharina believed her. And I, although I could easily have refuted the girl's sneaky lie, did nothing. A friendship was destroyed, but it had begun to crumble weeks or months earlier; she and I had just been dragging it along. Only the uncompromising hatred between two unhappy girls revealed traces of love, fatally wounded.

A few weeks later, the day came when I publicly turned against Katharina.

After school we all had to stay in class for another discussion on joining the socialist youth organization. Katharina was the only pupil who had refused to apply for admission. So we had to stay late just because of her, and because of her the teacher went over the same old arguments and slogans again. We sat yawning, resenting the waste of time, letting the words wash over us. When the teacher challenged us to take a position, we obediently mumbled whatever words she put in our mouths.

Katharina sat pale and ramrod-straight. The teacher pointed out that joining the youth group was a vote for world peace. Katharina asserted that she too was for peace.

But according to the teacher's reasoning, refusal to join the youth organization was tantamount to warmongering. This logic beat Katharina down and left her speechless.

The rest of us listened grumpily and without interest to the familiar phrases, just waiting to be released. Katharina's refusal was costing us our free time; her stubbornness seemed futile, and very uncomradely. We wanted to go home, but because of her we had to stay after school again.

On that day I raised my hand, turning toward Katharina as I did. I stood up and ridiculed the Christian superstitions of a certain classmate of ours. A stupid, witless remark, but the teacher and the other students laughed. Katharina blushed beet-red. Pleased with my success, I sat down. Suddenly Katharina got up, came over to my desk, and slapped my face. Instinctively I kicked her in the shins. We both yowled with pain and started to cry, and both of us were given a demerit in the class logbook. That was the last thing we had in common, for we had already begun wearing different hair styles some time earlier.

That summer, when we were supposed to make our joint decision on the issue of religion, Katharina and her mother left to join the three brothers in Lower Saxony. I was relieved when I heard about it. I told my father, almost proudly, that Katharina had betrayed the Republic.

That summer my parents bought me a red leather briefcase. I didn't want to show up at school in the district capital with a child's satchel on my back.

And now I was sitting in a room in the only hotel in G. and drinking beer. And I poured a bit of the yellowish, ice-cold liquid onto the frayed runner in front of the chair. A libation for a girl I had loved without reserve, as I would never be able to love again.

A year after Katharina's departure, my family also moved away from G. The daily train trip to the district capital had become too strenuous for me, and besides, Father had received a good offer from a machine factory in Magdeburg.

Not until two years later did I learn from my mother that there'd been another reason for our move. Uncle Gerhard, my father's cousin who lived in G. and often visited us, had been arrested. In December, when we'd already been in Magdeburg for four months, he was sentenced to five years in the penitentiary. Father had to appear as a witness at the trial.

Uncle Gerhard was much older than Father. He lived alone in an apartment crowded with old furniture. His wife died shortly after the war. It was rumored that she had committed suicide. Mother merely told me that she'd met a tragic end, and when I kept asking questions, she replied that it was wartime and many dreadful things had happened.

Uncle Gerhard was retired. Mornings he worked at the post office, sitting behind a counter selling stamps and magazines. Before I started school, I visited him almost every afternoon. We played cards or sang old songs while he accompanied us on a concertina. He knew lots of riddles and loved to tease me. When he pointed at me and, giggling, sang some mocking lines, he could bring me to the verge of tears. When I was five or six the prospect of becoming an old maid particularly terrified me, and Uncle Gerhard found this hilarious.

There she stands without a man
And thinks she'd rather die.
Next time grab one while you can
Lest fortune pass you by.

Afterwards he gave me candy, which quickly calmed me down.

As I got older I went to see Uncle Gerhard less frequently, but our relations were always warm. When I turned twelve, he showed me his will, which named me as his sole heir.

He was like a grandfather to me, and I think he regarded me as his foster child or grandchild. On my birthdays he always gave me money, which didn't please my parents; they would quarrel with him, which only deepened the understanding between us. He was seventy-two when he was convicted. He had helped the Nazis ferret out members of the Social Democratic and Communist parties in G., although he himself had been a Social Democrat since he was seventeen. It never came to light why he had done it, not even at his trial.

The court declared him an accessory to the murder of four persons. Six years after the war he told my father what he had done. At the trial my father testified that he hadn't reported Uncle Gerhard because he was a cousin, and an old man besides. The judge gave my father a reprimand.

I don't know what led my uncle to do it. He was a jolly, good-natured man easily moved to tears. I imagine the Nazis threatened him, and that he betrayed his comrades out of fear.

My whole world collapsed back then. My horror at the fascist terror, my tears over the *Diary of Anne Frank*, about the Jewish girl in hiding, suddenly seemed mendacious and hypocritical to me. I felt I had lost the right to be indignant about atrocities or to pity the victims.

At first I had a need to purge myself, to publicly declare my guilt. I wrote in school compositions that I was the niece of a Nazi criminal and shouldn't be permitted to mock the victims with my compassion. My parents and teachers, not knowing what to do, simply passed over my self-accusations in silence. In the twelfth grade one of my class-mates told me she considered my behavior affected. She said I shouldn't be so self-important; it made me seem ridiculous and high-flown. I contradicted her violently. But from then on, I kept quiet about it. At home no one mentioned Uncle Gerhard, not even me. If the topic of fascism came up, I said little or nothing. I realized that I was a problem, insoluble, impossible to get rid of, inexplicable. And I began to keep quiet so as not to annoy others.

Uncle Gerhard died in the third year of his prison term. Father rejected the inheritance, and the estate was auctioned off to benefit the city of G.

The hotel room became more inhospitable the longer I sat in the chair. The wallpaper was grubby. I was afraid that if I stared at it any more, tiny animals would come crawling out from behind it. I undressed. As I approached the bed, I stepped in something cold and wet. My libation. I found it so unpleasant that I went to the sink and held my foot under the lukewarm water for a long time. No, I had nothing to do with this town. The trip to G. was ill-conceived and stupid.

The next morning at breakfast the rolls were a day old, the coffee tasted of chicory and adding insult to injury, the manager came to our table twice to ask if everything was all right. Since he had an artificial arm or hand (all we saw were stiff fingers in a black leather glove), we assured him that everything was wonderful. I told Henry we should leave immediately, I was tired and jittery, and would he please spare me his ironic remarks. I said it in a friendly way so as not to offend him, and I think he understood.

We paid for our rooms and drove off. Since we had no particular plans, we decided to stop in Wörlitz. It was a warm, sunny, fall day. Groups of tourists were being herded through the large park. Like flocks of birds they suddenly alighted somewhere, loud and fluttering, and just as suddenly they disappeared.

Otherwise it was quiet. In the afternoon it rained, but soon the sun returned and brought out crowds of visitors. We walked from the palm garden to the grottos and continued on to the meadows along the Elbe. Here we were alone. We lay on the grass in our coats and sunned ourselves. I asked Henry what he remembered when he thought of his childhood. He replied that he never thought of it.

But sometimes, I said, sometimes our own past comes over us like an unwanted shadow. We can't keep it out of our later life.

I don't let it near me, he replied.

Why not? I asked.

He bent over me and looked into my eyes.

Because it's pointless, he said. Because it makes us incapable of living. And I don't need it, he added. I don't have any problems with myself.

That's hard to believe, I said.

He laughed out loud, kissed me, and said I could think whatever I liked. He said he was used to having women look for a deeper meaning in him. He didn't care.

Then we walked along the Elbe. When it got dark, we turned back. It was a dark night without stars, unrelieved by city lights. Not accustomed to such blackness, we stumbled and nearly fell several times before we found the car.

We drove into Wörlitz to have supper. The only restaurant open was too crowded, so we went to the railroad station and had salad and cheese in a grimy Mitropa cafeteria. There was a sharp smell of beer and stale cigarette smoke. Around ten we started back to Berlin.

On the entrance ramp to the highway we almost crashed into an oncoming car. Henry was driving fast, and the other car suddenly shot around the corner. We were in the wrong lane. I saw the headlights coming directly at me and screamed. The other car honked, loud, insistent. I grabbed onto the wheel to pull the car to the side. The other driver braked and swerved. Henry hit me in the face with the back of his hand. Then our car sped past the other. I turned around and saw the driver open the door and get out, his hand still on the horn. Then the car and the man disappeared, and we went tearing along a concrete gully that slid away beneath us as our headlights dug it out of the darkness ahead.

Neither of us said anything. I had reached for the wheel instinctively, or out of fear. I knew that Henry would get out of the way in time. It had happened quickly, too quickly for me to think. And I knew that Henry hadn't hit me by accident. It wasn't a reflex, a defensive reaction that also took him by surprise.

We sat in the car looking at the darkness ahead of us, only feebly pierced by the headlights. We said nothing. I was glad Henry didn't apologize or offer an explanation. I knew he wasn't one of those men who beat their wives or girlfriends, but I also know that at some time, in some particularly complicated or upsetting situation, every man will hit. He'll be able to control himself with other men, but not with women and children. It's not our helplessness that makes them do it, not the chance to demonstrate the power of the stronger over the weaker. That doesn't explain their self-discipline with members of their own sex. I've seen men insulted by other men. Mortally wounded by words, they sit smiling in their chairs. They struggle for composure, they get loud or very quiet, they stay polite or turn crude. But they don't hit. They're each other's equals; they don't hit with that condescending, almost trivial movement of the hand used to punish or prod an animal. Even when their confrontation becomes physical, they don't abandon the fairness accorded to others of equal rank. They strike only when the other person is ready to be struck. Ceremonial jockeying for position. A duel with internalized seconds. Sovereign equals in an honorable struggle.

But one hits a woman as one hits a dog, casually, in passing. A necessary educational technique for the benefit of the one who is hit. An embrace can follow the blow immediately. After all, it doesn't come out of hatred, it's just to set things straight.

It's a feeling of superiority, cultivated over centuries, almost innate by now, that brings a man to hit a woman. Even the most progressive, open-minded man will reach the point where he succumbs to his instinct of superiority. Then he's shocked at himself, at this attitude, in such contrast to his "real" attitude. Usually he'll apologize right away, feel angry with himself, indulge in self-analysis, which in turn provides him with some kind of explanation. Hinner once excused himself by saying that he had let himself go, and he was furious with me when I laughed at that. But he was right, it is a form of letting oneself go. The tamed beast of prey which suddenly, unexpectedly, and to everyone's mystification, dismembers its beloved. At least unconsciously they feel superior to us, and their hitting, no matter how much it startles them, has a pedagogical intent, it's an act of divine pedagogy. Intellectually they're capable of recognizing women as equals, as beings of the same rank, and they're willing to do so. But in their deeper selves they're still dominated by their masculine sense of self-worth, a weird mixture of inhibitions and arrogance.

One time when I went to see my friend Charlotte, I found Michael, her husband, in a state of despair. He, that good-hearted, permissive, understanding father, had struck his child. He, who wouldn't hurt a fly. He was horrified by his own behavior, railed at himself in my presence, and kept hauling the child onto his lap, kissing and caressing it and begging in the silliest way to be forgiven. The scene disgusted me. His sorrow over his deed seemed genuine, but what he was mourning was his own self-esteem, which had been damaged by that blow. He himself had smashed the image of civilized behavior that was so dear to him, and now he was lamenting the sight of the barbarian that had been revealed. With desperate talk and caresses he was demanding that the child give him back his civilized personality, so he could cast the barbarian back into the deep, dark recesses of the soul, the dungeons of our humanity. Poor, ridiculous men.

Henry said nothing. We drove back to Berlin without a word, and that was all for the best.

At the door to my apartment we said good-bye. He gave a wan and embarrassed smile. I calmly wished him a good night.

I wouldn't forget that blow, or forgive him for it. But I also knew I wouldn't think much about it. I was nearly thirty-nine now, too old to be astonished by something so trivial. When it rains, we get wet; I'm not a young girl anymore and I should be used to it. Everything runs on its usual course, perfectly normal. No reason to scream. Don't get hysterical. I want to remain what I am, a nice, very normal woman. Nothing happened.

The air in the room was stifling. I opened the window before I dropped into my easy chair.

10

. . . .

In November I was sick for two weeks. My back was bothering me, a disk. Nothing major, just painful. Exercises,
ultrasound treatment, and underwater massage didn't do
much good, or at least didn't make me feel better. A common health problem. The bones begin to dissolve, the joints
degenerate into dust. An evolutionary cycle, back to the

amphibians, the water creatures, the primal amoeba. The fact that the human race is retrogressing is still being more or less covered up. Organs that have long since become unusable are being replaced by fantastic inventions: cars and escalators, pacemakers and respirators, gold teeth, plastic prostheses, stainless steel plates, all more durable than the original bones. Nature perfected. The survival of mankind a matter of spare parts. Progress dependent on the flawless operation of the supply lines; procreation guaranteed by the polarity of male and female spare parts. The rest a question of magnetism.

Before my period began, I requested a sick leave. I knew I wouldn't be able to keep going otherwise.

I did a lot of walking, and every morning I went swimming for an hour in the municipal indoor pool. After breakfast I sat and listened to records, a soothing start to the day. I looked for a goldsmith to repair a little necklace of mine. Everywhere I went they tried to talk me out of it. Repairs are too much trouble. Twice I went to pick up Henry after work. The first time he was surprised; I'd never come there to meet him before.

He was leaving his office building with a colleague. The three of us went to a café on the Spree River. The colleague, a Herr Krämer, told incredible stories about his work and laughed heartily at his own jokes. I could tell he liked me; when I spoke, he fell silent and looked at me intently. Later he tried to figure out the relationship between Henry and me. At least, that's how I interpreted his invitation to celebrate New Year's with him. Henry was reserved, and I didn't know whether he felt uncomfortable being seen by a colleague with his "relationship." As we were leaving the café he reached for my hand, a first sign of our closeness, probably intended specifically for his colleague's benefit. The other man took note of it with a satisfied smile. When we parted, I caught the look of acknowledgment that passes from man to man: silent congratulations on Henry's choice. The knowing look of the connoisseur, the champagne expert, the horse lover. Henry scratched his neck. That gave him something to do, which meant he didn't have to react. I agreed to meet Herr Krämer for New Year's, although I knew I wouldn't be in Berlin. He'd get over it.

We walked through the city, looking in shop windows. Henry seemed edgy. The wind whipped up dust and old newspapers from the streets. When we passed a kiosk, I asked Henry whether he'd like to go to the theater. We couldn't find anything interesting, though. I suggested we stop somewhere to eat, but he said he didn't have time. He had to get to Dresden; his wife was expecting him. He hadn't wanted to mention it earlier. His older son was making trouble in school and his wife had asked him to come. I said he should leave right away; he should have told me. He nodded. I walked him to the subway. Suddenly he began to complain about his wife. In general he never spoke of her, but now he said that she was always calling up with some catastrophe, always demanding that he come to see her and the children. Things didn't seem to be working out with her boyfriend. She kept summoning Henry to Dresden every weekend. And after ten minutes we're already quarreling, he said bitterly.

Before he went into the subway, Henry pushed his hat to the back of his head and kicked out violently at some imaginary object. As we were saying good-bye, I saw that a button was missing from his shirt. I wondered why I noticed. I went back to my apartment, made supper, and ate in front of the television. After that I went to bed. Now that I was sick I had a great need for sleep.

In the second week the chief came to see me. It was the first time he'd been to my place. I'd never heard of his visiting a colleague, and when I opened the door and saw him standing there, I must have stared at him in complete amazement. He became embarrassed, and silently handed me a bouquet of flowers wrapped in paper. Then he took it back, hastily unwrapped it, and gave me the flowers— carnations—again. Gradually he regained his self-confidence. He found my room dreadful and promised to see to it that I got a decent apartment. I said I was satisfied with it and didn't need any more. We had coffee, and he made friendly remarks of no consequence. I didn't know why he'd come. I waited for him to give some reason for his visit.

He looked over my books and noted with disappointment that I had hardly anything but belles lettres. Didn't I read any professional literature, he wanted to know. I shook my head. Every so often I buy the journals, or a book on recent research that someone's recommended, but then I usually don't have the energy to read it. I said I hadn't felt the urge to do that for years now. Sometimes a sort of moral fervor about keeping informed would well up in me, but that was merely an impulse from the past, a throwback to an earlier enthusiasm, which soon faded. Besides, I couldn't see what good the literature might do me. It was merely the "scholarly approach," a humanistic model left over from bygone centuries. For the work at the hospital my university training was perfectly adequate, along with the things the doctors discussed among themselves or in the regular professional development courses. He said he couldn't understand my attitude. I knew what he meant, I replied. Sometimes I didn't understand it myself.

You have no self-discipline, he said. Your entire generation has no self-discipline.

He fiddled nervously with his shirt collar. Then he jumped up and exclaimed, Do you know that I haven't been sick for one single day in the last fifteen years, not one single day. Health, my dear, is a question of self-discipline. And I say that as a physician.

His broad bow tie with its blue pattern was askew. I told him I shared his opinion and would gladly hear from him how I could acquire this marvelous self-discipline. I myself regretted that I had so much less than he, but unless he could prescribe some in the form of an injection or a multivitamin supplement, I didn't see any hope for myself. He looked at me pityingly and said, It's not going to be easy for you. Your whole generation is going to have a hard time growing old.

That may be, I said, but I don't know what can be done about it.

You must practice self-discipline, my child, he said. I replied that it would just be illusory, it would soon fall apart. But he repeated several times that I should practice it.

He was dissatisfied with me, but that didn't bother me. He was an old man, and I felt he had the right to say these things. Maybe it was because I didn't dislike him. Besides, I really wasn't interested anymore.

Then he tried to make small talk, but he was no good at it. Probably he was too much of a pedagogue for casual conversation. When he left, I asked him whether he hadn't come for a specific purpose, with some message, some concern. Did I think he was that type? he asked. And at once I said, Yes.

Perhaps you're not so wrong, but this time I just came, he said with a smile. And then he added, Do pay us a visit some time—you know, my wife . . .

I said I knew, and would stop by soon.

Why had he come? I couldn't figure it out. He was a dear old man, a bit of a curmudgeon, a bit stiff and formal, but a good boss. He was something like an old-fashioned ladies' man, I thought, with secret rendezvous, little well-planned surprises, always impeccably dressed, scented with just the right after-shave. I was sure he'd picked out the carnations himself.

While I was washing the dishes, I remembered that my colleagues had very different stories to tell about him. Perhaps it was ill-will on their part, or else he had another, entirely different side. Perhaps his visit to me had been a daring breech in his self-discipline.

A day before I went back to work, Mother telephoned. I was just rearranging the kitchen, that is, I was moving some things around without gaining much extra room. She had called the hospital, and they had told her that I was sick. She wanted to know what was wrong, why I hadn't been in touch. I told her everything was fine. I promised to come for Christmas. She asked if I'd be alone. When I didn't reply, she said that if I wanted to bring a friend, it would be all right, of course. I asked how Father was doing, after which we said good-bye. Then she asked whether there was anything else, and then she said good-bye again. After that she gave me Father's love, and we said good-bye for the third time.

In the evening I went with Henry to visit acquaintances of his. I think they'd been at school together. It was tiring, and we were all bored. We didn't have anything to say to each other, so we talked about television programs. After a little while I said I had to leave. When I got up, Henry rose to accompany me. His acquaintances protested, and I said I could go alone. Henry sat down again. The next day he called me at the hospital and told me that the evening had taken an unpleasant turn. His acquaintances had been annoyed that I'd left so soon, after they'd gone to so much trouble with the preparations.

The second week in December I had a call from Michael, Charlotte's husband, who sounded upset and asked if he could come by. When he arrived, he told me that his father had been put into a nursing home. The old man hadn't wanted to go, but the neighbors had him committed while Michael was out of town on business. They wanted the old man's apartment for themselves. Michael hoped that I could help him get his father out. I called the doctor who had signed the committal papers, a man I knew only by name, and had a long conversation with him. The doctor said that Michael's father had been what they called a "no-heat" committal. At noon they had gone to the apartment to check on the complaint. They found him in bed, the place unheated, and everything in a mess. Also, the old man hadn't had anything hot to eat in several days. Everything seemed to favor a "no-heat" committal to a nursing home, and the doctor had done the paperwork immediately.

I asked him whether Michael's father had been in agreement. Emphasizing each word separately, he said that consent was not necessary when a person had been so seriously neglected.

Michael sat next to me and listened to the conversation. He whispered that I should tell the doctor that the neighbors had been eyeing the apartment and had used Michael's absence to get rid of the old man. The doctor said that was certainly possible; it had happened before. Some reports had even been made anonymously or under assumed names, and because of this the authorities checked every case carefully. But with Michael's father, it was simply a no-heat committal for the winter. The old man would be released in the spring, and he would keep his apartment in any case.

Then he spoke to Michael and encouraged him to get his father out of the institution and take him into his own home. Michael raised objections but vacillated. Finally he agreed. He would either move his father into his own apartment, or else let him live alone and go over every day to take care of him. Michael and the welfare doctor arranged a time to pick him up.

Michael seemed relieved, and I hoped he wouldn't regret the decision. I don't know whether I would let my mother or father come and live with me. It would be a strain, also complicated, because I'm on call at night so often.

After he left I called my parents. When Father answered the phone, I forgot what I wanted to say. I'd called because Michael's obvious attachment to his father had flustered me, but I could hardly tell my father that I was calling only because other people loved their parents.

I just wanted to ask how he was, I told him. He was fine, or so he said. He had nothing new to report; neither did I. We soon hung up.

In the middle of December it turned cold and began to snow. The snow didn't stay on the ground; the streets were slippery and dirty. During the day it never really got light.

The sky was like grimy cotton batting, and my room was always overheated. It didn't do much good to turn off the radiators. A favorable climate for cockroaches. When I got into the shower, I always looked carefully in the corners and other likely hiding places. Three years ago, roaches had spread through the whole building with unbelievable speed. All the floors were fumigated. Since then I haven't seen any, but I'm always afraid they may come creeping out again.

I received my annual package of home-baked Christmas bread from Mother. In the enclosed letter, spotted with fat and moist from the bread, she wrote that she was looking forward to my visit and that my sister was coming for Christmas too. Father was having problems with his lungs again, and she with her leg, and what did I want for Christmas? She had written it on a piece of lined paper torn out of a school notebook. She always wrote on pages torn out of notebooks. She had started doing it when my sister and I were in school, but that was thirty years ago. Why did she go on buying school notebooks just to tear out the sheets for her lists and her short, awkward letters?

On the Saturday before Christmas I was awakened by birds twittering. I had trouble waking up, and it took me a long time to realize that it was birds making all the noise. It seemed unreal; there are no birds near our building. I lay in bed with my eyes shut and thought about it. I was relieved when it finally came to me that they must be Frau Rupprecht's birds, but at the same moment I realized that I'd never heard them so loud and clear. Suddenly I was wide awake. I had a feeling something had happened. I got up quickly and took a shower, dressed and went to her door. When I rang the bell, all I could hear was the birds. I rang again and again and knocked on the door. I heard doors opening behind me. A woman asked what was wrong. I gave some answer or other. Then I went back into my apartment. I tried to fight my growing sense of anxiety. The chirping continued. It seemed to me it was getting louder. Something's happened: the thought kept circling in my head, like a millwheel I couldn't stop. Something's happened, said the voice in my head, over and over again, as I put on water for coffee.

I considered what might have happened, and then told myself I was crazy. The birds must always have chirped that way; I just hadn't paid attention. Now that I'd noticed, I was concentrating on it too much, that was all.

I lit a cigarette and sat down. I put it out and left the apartment. I took the elevator to the ground floor and rang for the superintendent. I asked him to come upstairs and open Frau Rupprecht's door. I tried to explain, but he said grumpily that he couldn't break into an apartment just because someone had a feeling. He was wearing pants but no shirt, and the suspenders were tight over his chest with its mat of gray hair. His bare feet were in felt slippers.

I wouldn't leave—I knew I couldn't get rid of my anxiety any other way. He finally agreed to come along. He went into his apartment and came back wearing a shirt and carrying a bunch of keys. In the elevator he growled that I'd have to take the responsibility, he wasn't paid for such things. I promised to give him five marks. He nodded with satisfaction but said he hadn't meant it that way.

The little vestibule of Frau Rupprecht's apartment smelled of bird feed and sand. The superintendent said such things shouldn't be allowed. He meant the stench.

When we opened the door to the room, Frau Rupprecht was sitting in her chair looking at us. The tiny spots of her eyes, little black mirrors in a thicket of wrinkles, were directed at us. The superintendent explained why we'd come in. Then he broke off and said, Shit! Frau Rupprecht was dead. The smell in the room was oppressively sweet. It was all I could do to stand it.

Most of the birds were twittering and fluttering excitedly in their cages. A few were hunched on their perches or on the sand-strewn bottoms of the cages: perhaps they were ill. The superintendent went to the balcony door and opened it. I tried to close Frau Rupprecht's eyes, but couldn't. The lids had disappeared into the wrinkles of the eye sockets. She was cold to the touch. When I was about to try again, the superintendent said I shouldn't change anything.

I wanted to give the birds food and fresh water, but he wouldn't allow it. He made me leave the apartment when he did. He locked it carefully behind him, looking at me with distrust. He said he would see to everything that had to be done, he had experience. If I knew any acquaintances of Frau Rupprecht's, I could notify them. I didn't answer. He pulled a single squashed cigarette out of the pocket of his shirt. It flared up when he lit it, because some of the tobacco was sticking out.

At noon the police arrived, and a doctor. At least, I assumed so from the way the superintendent was talking to them in the hall. I didn't go out. I waited for them to call me. Nobody did.

Two hours later, attendants appeared with a stretcher. That, too, I deduced from the conversations I overheard. As they were carrying the body out, they bumped into my door. At first I was about to open it, I thought they needed my help. But I didn't move.

The door between my apartment and the little vestibule was open. I heard every word, every tone of voice, every sound. Frau Rupprecht's last words to her neighbors.

A man, presumably one of the attendants, swore and shouted down the corridor: The woman's been dead for three days; you can croak in this building and nobody gives a damn.

In the evening the superintendent rang my bell. He gave me the key and asked whether I could take care of the birds for the time being. I went into the apartment, washed out the bowls, and filled them with fresh water and bird seed. There were fourteen cages hung all around the walls. Of twenty-three birds, two were dead. I wrapped them in a newspaper I found on the kitchen counter.

It took almost an hour to finish.

I didn't feel right doing this. I kept thinking Frau Rupprecht would suddenly appear and I would have to explain what I was doing in her apartment. I regretted that I hadn't managed to close her eyes. The dead seem less aggressive to me when their eyes are closed.

When I was done with everything, I took the bundle of newspaper with the dead birds and threw it down the garbage chute. In my own apartment I washed my hands, scrubbing them thoroughly with a brush.

Two days later the superintendent came to get the key back. He couldn't tell me anything about Frau Rupprecht's funeral. No relatives had turned up. He planned to store her furniture and belongings in the basement until he heard something.

He asked whether I could take the birds, or at least some of them, for now. I said I was going away, and he replied bitterly that he understood. No one wanted to take those birds of death. I asked where Frau Rupprecht's corpse was. He was still bitter.

I don't know, he said. And with a slight grin, he added: Where should it be?

Until late that night I could hear him cleaning up next door. I turned up the television. I was relieved that he had taken back the key. I felt uncomfortable going into Frau Rupprecht's empty apartment in the evening to take care of her birds. Birds of death, as he said. I found it an invasion of her privacy. They were her birds, she should have taken them with her.

Two days before Christmas I did my shopping. At a gourmet shop I picked out, pretty much at random, bottles of fine schnapps, jars of seasonings, brightly colored tins of meat and fancy vegetables. When the saleswoman had piled up my mountain of goods, she asked whether that would be all. I hope so, I said, and paid for it. I hoped I had bought enough items to cover everyone the coming holiday forced me to think of. Happy holidays, the saleswoman said.

At home I would wrap everything and go through my address book, which was cluttered with little pencil checks next to the names. Names of people from all the past Christmases for whom I'd tortured my brain thinking up so-called personal gifts. Today I no longer even look for personal gifts, anything will do. Besides, I don't know what a personal gift is. I think if I really gave someone a personal gift, it would scare him to death. I don't know what a personal gift for myself would be, either. But I'm sure that if it were really personal, I would burst into tears. At least I'd know then what sort of person I am. To this day I haven't figured that out, and I don't even know whether I'm interested in doing so. I probably have another thirty years to live, at least according to the statistics. And I'm not sure knowing who I really am would help me get through those years. I live with myself without asking a lot of questions. Like every normal person, I'm sometimes afraid of going out of my mind. When you've seen that happen to one or two people you know, you realize how quickly it can come about. You can't be too sure you won't be next. And I'm convinced that the surest way to go crazy is to start trying to figure out who you really are, who this person is that you're living with. Psychiatry has achieved a few successes in our century, but then it's had unprecedented numbers of patients to work with. I don't particularly dislike psychiatry or neuropsychology; on the other hand, I don't particularly like them either. I've noticed that you can find anything in anybody if you start looking.

Happy holidays, the saleswoman said. When I was about to return the greeting, she was already busy with the next customer. Her face still wore that grimace of slightly forced amiability as she piled up another mountain of canned goods and bottles. The personal gifts of the next customer.

On Christmas Eve I went out for lunch with Henry. He'd be with his family for Christmas, but we didn't say anything about it. He didn't want to think about the scenes with his wife just yet. We planned to spend New Year's together in Magdeburg, at my parents'.

After lunch I set out. Henry saw me to my car. As we were saying good-bye, he pressed a little package into my hand. Please, please don't, I thought, and smiled at him.

He looked after me, his hat pushed back, as I drove off. I watched him in the rearview mirror until he disappeared behind trees, cars, pedestrians, dissolved into the damp, dirty gray of the asphalt.

11

. . . .

The day after Christmas I told Mother that I wanted to take some pictures and wouldn't be back until evening. Mother asked what was left to photograph, I already had pictures of the whole area. I said that the landscape was constantly changing. I could see her feelings were hurt. She probably guessed that I was bored at home and simply wanted a reason to get away. She sensed that, and she certainly also sensed that I knew she knew. So I was grateful that she didn't say anything more and just let me go. She packed up coffee and sandwiches for me, although I'd asked her not to go to any trouble.

I'd been bored since I got there. On Christmas Eve I didn't arrive until late. They had everything ready, and after the usual reproaches, which weren't meant to be taken seriously, we went into the Christmas room. I admired the tree because I knew Father had been decorating it all day, and he was pleased. We gave each other the presents, and for a moment I was sorry to have bought mine with so little care. But they were both pleased, or acted as if they were. Everything was expensive and of high quality; that was something at least.

Later, as usual, we sat in front of the television. Mother insisted on talking, which disturbed Father. We drank wine to celebrate the day, as Mother put it. (At home, wine is drunk every evening to celebrate the day.) At some point Mother cried, I didn't know why, and probably she wasn't sure either. No one needs a particular reason not to cry, so why should you need one for crying?

Since the only thing on was children's choirs and string quartets, Father turned off the television. Then they wanted to know how I was. I made an effort to tell them something I thought might interest them, or at least entertain them.

I didn't want to be the first to go to bed again, because that would hurt their feelings. So I stayed up and tried to keep awake.

Late in the evening Irene, my sister, phoned. Originally

she had promised to be there for Christmas Eve, but two days ago she had called and said she couldn't make it until Christmas Day.

On the telephone she was very cheerful, a little drunk, I think. She wished us all the best, and one after the other we took the phone to wish her the same. When it was my turn she said, giggling, that I was going to be very surprised when she showed up. I said I'd be glad to see her; we hadn't seen each other since last Christmas. I had to promise not to get mad at her, she said. When I asked what she meant by that, she hung up.

We stayed in the living room a while longer. Mother talked, and Father kept asking whether we didn't want a bite to eat. Later he tried again to find something interesting on the television. Then he asked if we should play a game, but Mother and I didn't feel like it, so we went to bed.

At lunchtime the next day Irene arrived with Hinner. He was working as a surgeon here in the district hospital, but I hadn't known he was coming. And though Mother acted surprised, I sensed that she'd invited him. Since our divorce I hadn't been able to stop her from arranging un-expected meetings. She hoped we would get back together, because she'd been proud of us, or rather of our marriage, or of the good stories she could tell about us. We had both been ambitious enough to be quite successful. Our marriage was certainly the kind mothers dream of for their daughters, and deep down she had simply never accepted the fact of our divorce. It didn't fit in with her dream.

But this Christmas appearance of Irene and Hinner fit even less.

She'd invited Irene, and of course she'd also invited Hinner. But no more than the rest of us could she have imagined that the two of them would show up together.

Irene works as a teacher in Rostock. She's married to an engineer, whom she treats condescendingly and with whom she is always put out. Her husband does seem pale and insignificant, and in our presence she acts as if he were a weak, dull-witted failure. She behaves disgustingly, and her husband sits there looking wounded and uncomfortable, while Father, Mother, and I act as though we aren't listening. They have a daughter, probably four or five now, who unfortunately resembles her father.

Her husband and child had stayed in Rostock; I don't know what story she told them. A few days ago she called Mother and said she was going to spend the holidays alone and didn't want to be asked any questions.

Mother's face broke out in hectic red blotches when she saw them together. She never becomes jittery or loud when something's too much for her. She remains quiet, looks at us amiably, and those red blotches appear on her cheeks.

We greeted each other. Hinner kissed me on the cheek. Then we sat down to lunch. At the table we all talked very uninhibitedly, almost unbelievably so. Only Father didn't seem to notice anything. He was surprised that Irene and Hinner had arrived at the same time, and asked about my sister's husband and daughter. She gave minimal replies.

While they were in the kitchen doing dishes, Irene asked Mother not to say anything to her husband. He would probably phone and ask about her, and Mother should say she wasn't there at the moment. She would tell him everything herself, later, when she got back. Mother nodded quietly and bent her head over the sink. With brief, energetic motions she scrubbed at a plate. Gradually the red blotches reappeared on her cheeks again.

I took the dishes into the living room. Hinner was sitting in the easy chair smoking a cigar. When I came in, he stood up. He tried to help me, but didn't know what to do. He stood beside me, uncertain. He asked how I was and what was happening at work. Then he told me he'd been head physician since September. I acted surprised. Years ago he was always complaining about the way promotions were handled at his hospital. He had few prospects of getting ahead, and he was bitter and hurt, full of sarcasm. So I was all the more amazed now, even though Mother had already told me about the promotion. Hinner noticed my reaction and must have remembered too. He said that a number of things had changed for the better at the hospital in the last two years. He was getting along well with the director and even accompanied him to medical congresses now. They knew they had a good thing in him. I asked whether he'd joined the Party. He said yes. Then he added that it wasn't the way I thought; he had considered it carefully for a long time. I interrupted him to say I didn't think anything. He sat down again. When I looked at him, he asked whether I was angry. I asked why, and he said, Because I'm with your sister.

What business is that of mine? I said agreeably.

He said he was glad I was so reasonable about it. I was a good sport, and actually we'd always gotten along well. I replied that I didn't think I was a good sport, but I had nothing to do with this business. It was strictly between him and my sister. He got up and made an awkward attempt to stroke my cheek, repeating that I was a decent sort.

When I went back into the kitchen, my sister was crying

and my mother's eyes were red. Without a word I dried the glasses. At some point Mother broke the silence and said we should remember that it was Christmas, we should try not to make each other miserable. Then my sister asked me whether I also thought she had taken Hinner away from me. I said no, we'd been divorced for years; there was nothing more between us, and as far as I was concerned it was perfectly all right for her to sleep with him. My sister replied sharply that it wasn't a question of her sleeping with him, it was a question of their loving each other. I replied that I didn't know what it was a question of for her, but I could well imagine what it was a question of for Hinner. She cried again, and I wondered why I was being so mean to her. It had been absolutely unnecessary to say that. Why did I have to hurt her? Why did it bother me that she was with him?

I tried to apologize, to offer some explanation, but it didn't work. She gave me a furious look. Mother repeated mechanically: Be nice to each other, children, it's Christmas.

At teatime we talked about relatives. Mother chattered frantically, jumping from one subject to the other. My sister sulked and said nothing. And Hinner, ill at ease, perspired. At seven the two of them left. When they set out together, Father finally realized what was going on. His face turned almost gray as he said good-bye. I felt sorry for him. He couldn't understand or approve of this. In earlier days he would have pounded the table or started to shout, but he hasn't done that sort of thing for a long time. He bottles everything up inside. He sat down silently in front of the television set in the living room and could not be drawn into conversation. The skin over his knuckles was white.

We went to bed early. I heard Mother talking and talking

to Father in their bedroom, begging him to say something, anything. Since she kept asking him, I assumed that he was refusing to speak even to her.

I tried to think through my present relationship with Hinner. I couldn't discover any bond at all between us. In fact, often I didn't think about him for weeks and months. We had nothing to do with each other, and I couldn't understand why his involvement with my sister disturbed me. Why should I be disgusted by something that didn't concern me, that no longer touched me? Why did I feel humiliated? Dissatisfied with myself, I went to sleep.

We spent the day after Christmas very quietly. Somehow or other we got through it. In a chastened mood.

In the afternoon Aunt Gerda and Uncle Paul came over. The two men talked about politics, and Mother pressed me to talk about my work in Berlin.

That evening there was a call from Hannes, the engineer in Rostock, my sister's husband. Mother answered the phone. She asked about her grandchild. She signed to me that I should come to the phone and talk to him, but I shook my head. I went out of the room with Aunt Gerda and closed the door behind us. I knew it made her uncomfortable to lie to him about my sister in front of me.

Later Mother said hello to us from Hannes. I glanced over at Father. He didn't look up. I knew he was seething. If he were religious he would certainly curse my sister in grand Old Testament style.

The next day I drove out of town and took pictures. It was cold, and soon I felt frozen through. There was no café anywhere to get warm in. Even so, I didn't start home until darkness was falling.

I was annoyed that I had come to my parents'. We didn't

have anything to say to each other. And I knew that I would come again next year, and the year after that, and so on until death did us part. I would drive out here again and again, I would always be annoyed with myself, and I would never find the courage to end a relationship that had died long ago.

In the evening the three of us sat and talked. We talked about my childhood and about people we knew when we lived in G. Father was jolly and more sociable than I'd ever seen him, and Mother seemed happy. I was surprised that we had such different memories. A period that had frightened and oppressed me seemed to her carefree and full of droll jokes and anecdotes. They must have been happy while I was so unhappy. We had never understood each other.

It was a pleasant evening, almost lovely. There was just a brief moment of embarrassment when Mother asked what I was going to do the next day, and I told her I was going out to take pictures again.

Before we went to bed we hugged and kissed each other. Like old times, so long ago that I can't believe they ever existed.

On Sunday Henry arrived. With his usual wide-brimmed hat, he wore a broadly checkered brown suit. I'd never seen it before and almost doubled over with laughter. I told him he looked like the master of ceremonies in a second-rate variety show. He said it was his Sunday suit and he was hoping to make an impression. As we were going into the house, he stroked my buttocks and whispered that we should go to bed right away so we could make love.

Mother was ecstatic that Henry had come. She saw it as a token of trust, a proof of her and my unbroken, loving relationship. There were no secrets between mother and daughter, my life was still her life, and Henry's visit proved it. She bustled around him, brought out cake and cookies, and kept asking what she could offer him. I think she liked him.

Father talked to Henry about his work. Since Henry answered seriously and thoughtfully, Father was satisfied. He's only interested in politics and work, and he doesn't appreciate it when people speak lightly about either. He doesn't trust our generation; he thinks we lack a sense of responsibility. He fears that we'll fritter away all the things his generation values. He's disappointed in us, and very alarmed at how little we correspond to his ideas of what we should be. Sullen and annoyed, he takes note of what the new generation has in store for him.

When Mother inquired whether Henry had been married, and he replied that he was married and had two children, she and Father had to swallow hard again. He added that he was separated from his wife, but that didn't help much. The old folks were getting quite a buffeting this Christmas.

In the evening we played bridge. Mother was a woman transformed, and I knew she wanted him to like her. She was already beginning to fight for this potential son-in-law. She wanted to see her daughters happy, happy in the only way she could picture. Then later, in bed (Mother had asked me where Henry should sleep; she would have preferred him to sleep in the living room, but she didn't say anything when I answered, With me, of course), Henry told me that his wife had threatened him. Only vaguely, and he couldn't actually repeat what she'd said. Something about she couldn't go on living this way, and she didn't want to get divorced either, and then a vague, ambiguous threat. I asked him whether it disturbed him. He said he couldn't answer, he just didn't know. He caressed me and said: What worries me are the children.

We lay side by side and said nothing. We touched each other gently and smoked. We were following our own thoughts, contented and yet filled with uncertain, oppressive fears.

On New Year's Eve I helped Mother with the preparations. Henry went out with Father to the little garden behind the house. He told me later that they worked with the lathe in the shed.

After lunch Henry and I walked into town. It was a clear, sunny afternoon. Snow had fallen during the night, and now it lay trampled and dirty in the streets. Children and young people were standing in the doorways. They threw firecrackers after us and then ran shouting into the buildings, or sometimes stood there and waited for our reaction, looking bored.

It was warm, and we walked with our coats open. Henry asked what I expected of him. I didn't understand what he meant and looked at him perplexed.

I mean, he said, what do you picture happening with us?

I said I didn't give it much thought.

That's good, he said, I don't want to disappoint you. But I don't want to be disappointed either.

I replied that I was of the same opinion. And then he said, somewhat mysteriously, Let's hope so.

In a church a vesper service was taking place. We sat down in the last pew and listened. Apart from us there were only a few old people there. The priest kept looking over at us. Soon I got the feeling we were disturbing him. We didn't belong there, so we left.

On the way home we met many couples. The women

were wearing long dresses under their fur coats, and many had glittery ornaments in their hair. They wished us a happy new year, and we nodded to them.

On the sidewalk in front of the travel agency, children were playing in a burned-out car. The roof was missing. The door frames, twisted and covered with rust and blistered enamel, pointed threateningly at the sky. On our street corner a young woman was standing and crying in a whining sort of way. The tears cut colorful tracks down her heavily made-up face. She was leaning against the wall of the building and kept banging her pocketbook against her boots. Gold stars and red moons were glued to her puffy cheeks, and the tears had to make their way around them. A few steps away, a little man with a broken nose, like a boxer, stared at the pavement in disgust. The two were talking loudly without looking at each other. The woman said plaintively that he was a filthy pig, and he calmly offered to smash her face in.

As we passed, Henry wished them a happy new year. The man said in the same impassive voice, Right, buddy. Beat it.

In front of our house we turned to look at them. They were still standing on the corner.

In the evening Uncle Paul and Aunt Gerda came over, and later my sister and Hinner as well. We drank a lot, and Father quarreled with my uncle, who kept laughing at him.

Hinner wanted to speak to me alone. We went into the kitchen. He didn't say anything, and I asked what he wanted. Finally he asked me whether I hated my sister now. I said no. He said she felt humiliated, and I should make some kind of conciliatory gesture. Then he laughed softly and said that after all, I had loved him at one time, and my parents had also been pleased with him. So everyone should approve if he moved in with my sister now. I wanted to tell him that we were all positively delighted, but I didn't. Then he said he hadn't changed, didn't I agree? When we came back into the living room, my sister looked at me so humbly that it pained me. I smiled at her and she seemed relieved. Toward eleven o'clock my sister and Hinner said good-bye. They were supposed to stop off and see some friends.

At midnight we had toasts with champagne, and my uncle kissed Mother and me. Aunt Gerda demanded that Henry kiss her, which he did to her satisfaction, though at first he smiled awkwardly and hung back. Then Henry went out on the balcony and set off some firecrackers he had brought from Berlin. He had spent a fortune on them, and now, quite carried away, he lit one after the other. It was remarkable how much he enjoyed firing off his noisemakers and rockets.

Toward one, I got Mother to bed. She'd fallen asleep on the sofa and was gently snoring. When I waked her, she protested that she hadn't been asleep, she was wide awake, but she did let me take her to the bedroom. Then I went to bed too. At some point Henry came in. I was already half asleep. He lay down beside me and began to caress me. I said I was tired and had been asleep already. He growled something and left me alone.

On New Year's Day we had breakfast late, then drove back to Berlin. On the highway Henry tried to chase my car. He passed me and fell behind again on purpose. I refused to play his game.

In the mailbox I found New Year's cards and a letter

from Charlotte Kramer inviting me to spend New Year's
with them.

In the evening I went out to eat with Henry. I wanted
to talk to him about his wife, but he didn't want to, and
I dropped it. It was his problem, and I couldn't help.

The next day I went to the hospital early. Carla described
her New Year's party, and I acted as though I were listening.
Office hours began at nine.

12

. . . .

The next months passed; actually that was all that happened.
I went to work, and at home I was too tired to do anything
but read or watch television. I saw Henry two or three times
a week. Our relationship had settled down. It was gradually
becoming a habit, and quite bearable. Sometimes I didn't

see him for over a week. I wanted it that way, to keep us from getting into a rut, but I didn't really believe it.

A new tenant had moved into Frau Rupprecht's apartment, an officer in the army. I rarely saw him.

In February I turned forty. Mother came to visit; she spent half the day on the train just to be with me on my birthday for two hours. She gave me a blouse, and we went to a café. She said that my sister and Hinner would be getting engaged in the summer, if the divorce was final by then. The idea of an engagement struck me as ridiculous, but it didn't really interest me one way or the other. Father wasn't well, but Father hadn't been well for several years now. Mother asked what Henry had given me. When I said he had no idea it was my birthday, she was astonished. But she calmed down when I told her that we were still together. Then she wanted to know what she should do after Father died. I thought she was trying to tell me that she'd like to move in with me, so I was evasive and couldn't find much to say. Then she slapped herself on the mouth and said it was a sin to talk about such things; after all, Father was still alive.

In the evening I took her to the station. From the platform I could see her, a sad old woman, sitting behind the grubby window and asking me with a smile to trust her.

Once back home I tried to make myself realize that I was now forty, but I was not inspired. It was insignificant, nothing had changed. I wished that something would happen, that something would change, but I couldn't say what it should be.

In March daylight savings time began. Clocks were set forward an hour, and that was about the most exciting thing that happened in my life during these months. It didn't

affect me, but still it was an intrusion on time, an inter-
ruption of its regular, unwavering course. My life doesn't
have radical intrusions like that. It runs along with the
stupidity of a plumb bob, with the unchanging movement
of a pendulum, like the one in Uncle Gerhard's old clock
in G. A movement that leads nowhere, holds no surprises,
no deviations, no daylight savings times, and no irregular-
ities, and whose only sensational moment is when everything
eventually comes to a stop.

In the fall the clocks would be turned back again.

The turbulent event would then be smoothed over and
synchronized with my life. By fall, at the latest, everything
would return to its routine.

On my days off I sometimes drove outside the city. I
wanted to take photographs, but it was getting harder and
harder to find suitable subjects. I had the feeling I had
already photographed everything. Maybe I was upset by
compartments already crammed with pictures. Even at home
there wasn't room for my passion for quiet landscapes. I
would have had to fire myself up to go through the old
photos, then destroy most of them, but I didn't have the
strength. So I often came back without having taken a single
picture. It was a personal defeat that upset and bewildered
me, all the more because I saw how unimportant it was.

Occasionally I went to visit friends, though I usually
regretted it afterwards. Either we had little in common and
the conversation dragged, or I was afraid of getting involved
in their lives. I'm not interested in other people's problems
anymore. I have problems of my own that can't be solved.
Everybody has problems of their own that can't be solved.
Why talk about them? I know there are thousands of arguments in favor of doing precisely that, but it's never

helped me. I find it oppressive. I'm not a garbage pail for people's hopelessly tangled stories. I don't feel stable enough. I avoid spending more than an hour with Anne, the colleague who's regularly raped by her husband. I avoid meeting her anywhere but in public, in restaurants and cafés. That forces her to preserve at least a semblance of decorum. She can't let herself go and shower me with the details of her husband's shabbiness and messed-up psyche. I've never visited her at home and never will (except perhaps in the ambulance, in case this accumulation of banalities explodes some day, and I have the misfortune to be on call).

Until now I've managed to dodge the invitation to visit my chief and his wife. I'm afraid of being ambushed by him. I don't believe the sympathy with which he's stalking me is completely selfless. I can practically smell the ulterior motives behind his kindness: one day I'll ring his bell unsuspectingly, and after an hour in his easy chair, I'll be hopelessly trapped in the pit of his problems, inside another aching soul. It wouldn't give me any pleasure to have the respect and the bit of ambivalent love I feel for the old man reduced to ridiculous pity. I sense that he has problems, and I hope I never hear about them. I have problems too, and Anne has problems, and my parents, and Hinner, and my sister. And Henry's wife has problems. (Today, now that Henry's dead, she still has problems, but different ones. I don't want to know about those either.) Only Frau Rupprecht has no problems. Not anymore, although now the building superintendent does have a few.

I didn't discuss Henry's problems with him. He hinted at a few, and others I suspect. We succeeded brilliantly at avoiding them. The most intimate question we asked was: How are things? And according to our mutual agreement, neither of us had to reply. No need to worry about uncomfortable surprises. We won't importune one another with unpleasantness. We won't crush a nice relationship with insoluble difficulties. We're glad to give up this particular enrichment of our relationship. We're fine. No matter when we see one another, each of us is fine. We can rely on that, a secure island in a sea of personal problems. How are you? Fine. Otherwise stay at home and scream at the walls. When we see each other, Henry's fine, I'm fine. I'm not happy, but then I'm not unhappy either. I'm content, and that's saying a lot. And I'm content with this wordless agreement that makes our relationship simple and pleasant.

Henry died on April 18th. We'd seen each other just the day before. I had a cup of coffee with him before I left for the hospital. Two days later, I learned that he was dead. It was Frau Luban who rang my bell to tell me. I don't know how she had found out. She told me how, but I forgot or wasn't listening. She rang the bell, and then she said, I have bad news for you. Herr Sommer is dead. I thought you'd want to know.

I won't forget the expression in her eyes, a mixture of sympathy and brazen curiosity. She tried to come in, but I prevented her. I was too stunned to take in what she was telling me. Frau Luban attempted to hold my arm and lead me into my room. Somehow I managed to stop her. She said something I didn't understand. Then she asked whether she could be of any help. I looked at her and said: No. She remained standing in front of me. Then I said, Thank you, and slammed the door shut.

I sat down in my room and lit a cigarette. I thought about what Frau Luban had said to me. I had the feeling I had to come to some decision. It made me nervous that I was just sitting and smoking, but I had no clear idea what I should do. I didn't question the news for a moment, which I find hard to believe today. I felt no need to confirm it. The news of Henry's death didn't come as a surprise. I can hardly explain it to myself, but I wasn't surprised. Henry died unexpectedly, suddenly, out of the blue. It was terrible, but not surprising. I had had no premonition of his death, nor any fear of it, the news hit me without warning. But it didn't surprise me, and this seemed strange to me, disturbing.

Henry had been killed in a fight.

The morning after the visit from Frau Luban, I called Herr Krämer, Henry's colleague whom I'd met once. He liked me, he had tried to flirt with me. After that I had spoken with him several times when I called to speak to Henry.

I asked him when Henry's funeral would be, but he couldn't say; the body hadn't been released yet. I shuddered. Then he asked whether I was still on the line. I hastened to answer him. We agreed to meet after work at a restaurant.

When he arrived, he scanned all the tables, searching for me. His eyes passed over me twice; he didn't recognize me. I waved to him. He was pale and seemed distraught. (He made no attempt to flirt.) He kept grinning, a nervous smile, he was ill at ease. I didn't understand why. Then he told me. He had witnessed Henry's death. They'd gone to a bar to have a beer. A bunch of young guys made fun of Henry's hat, but Henry and he ignored them. Then one of the boys reached for the hat, and Henry blocked him. They began calling each other names. Henry offered to beat him up, and they went outside. Henry gave Herr Krämer the hat before he left. The other boys went out too, and Herr

Krämer followed. Henry and the boy, surrounded by the others, were standing a few steps away from the building. Henry had his fists in the air and was dancing around in front of the boy.

He used to be a boxer, did you know that?

I hadn't known.

Henry danced like a pro, and the boys laughed at him. He feinted into the air, as if he were warming up. Then the boy struck. Henry fell over. He fell backwards, stiff as a board. The boy must have had something like brass knuckles.

Herr Krämer ran over to Henry. His eyes were closed and he wasn't moving. There was a small cut in the skin above his left temple, and he was bleeding a little. Herr Krämer thought he was unconscious. In fact Henry was already dead.

The boys stood around him until one of them ran away, and then the others also disappeared. One boy told Herr Krämer he should keep his trap shut, otherwise he'd be next. People came out of the bar and asked what had happened. Herr Krämer told them to call a doctor and the police. He was still holding the felt hat. By this time he suspected that Henry might be dead. Later he was questioned and sent home. The next morning the police came to get him at work. They had all the boys in a lineup at the station, and he was supposed to identify them. The boy who had struck Henry was crying. He was seventeen. Most of them were minors, none was older than twenty. Then Herr Krämer was told he could go. The officer who saw him to the door asked why he hadn't intervened. He said that everything had happened so fast. Henry had smiled when he offered to beat the boy up. He'd gone outside looking bemused, and Herr Krämer hadn't believed he really meant to fight.

I blame myself now, Herr Krämer said, but believe me, it was his fault. I couldn't do anything.

I understand, I said.

He kept looking at me hopefully, as if I could absolve him of guilt. A guilt he was imagining and therefore could not escape without great difficulty.

Since I said nothing, he began playing with his beer glass. He looked down at his hands as he murmured, What a terrible thing. For me too, it's a terrible thing.

I nodded. He couldn't tell me anything about the funeral. The police hadn't released the body. I knew it might take weeks before Henry could finally be buried.

As I said good-bye, he asked whether we couldn't see each other again. After all, we'd both lost a friend. He looked helpless.

It wouldn't do us any good, I said in a friendly tone.

Then I left. I walked quickly because I was afraid he would follow. I went so fast I lost my breath. I found it ridiculous that I was running away.

During the following days I thought a lot about Henry. My mind always circled back to him. I tried to think what kind of person he'd been, but I couldn't decide. It was a spongy, unclear sort of thinking, a dull, unfocused brooding.

I continued to work, but at home I just sat around.

There was nothing about him in the papers. I hadn't expected there would be. The case was solved, there was nothing to clear up.

The funeral took place a month later, in the middle of May. I didn't feel any need to go, but I went nevertheless.

I wasn't feeling especially well around this time, I was depressed. I wasn't mourning Henry, it was probably just self-pity. I felt abandoned, left in the lurch. I had to get used to living completely alone again.

At the end of May, an old man moved into Henry's apartment. It was strange when, for the first time since Henry's death, I heard a key turn inside his apartment. I stood still and watched as the door opened and a strange man walked out.

The new tenant has a chronic catarrh. When he comes along the corridor, you can hear his dry, hacking cough. He's friends with an older woman from our floor. The two of them often leave the building together. They probably go to the cemetery; they always carry a plastic bag and a little watering can.

13

....

Now, half a year after Henry's burial, I've gotten used to being alone again. Things are fine with me, or at least good enough. There's nothing I lack. In four or five years I'll be promoted to head physician. The chief will back me, he's hinted at that. At some point I'll have to pay him that visit, and I'm sure it won't even be that bad. I like him in a strange, ambiguous way. I know that many people at the hospital can't stand him. He has the reputation of being dogmatic, arrogant, and cynical. Occasionally he behaves that way to me too. I think he likes playing the monster. It probably simplifies many decisions for him. I hope we can retain some formality in our dealings with each other. I hope he doesn't get sentimental and start telling me his problems. I don't want to hear about them.

Otherwise I'm content with my work, though it isn't what I thought it would be. I find it all the more strenuous because it goes along so routinely, without any particular stresses, excitements, or fun. I'll get through the next two decades all right.

I no longer have many desires, and I know I won't be able to fulfill the ones I do have. But I have a few specific fears, and they keep me fully occupied.

I hope I get through menopause without difficulty. I know I won't like the hot flashes. That I dread. I'm already familiar with the waves of heat that wash over me when I'm physically exhausted and depleted. I hate having to deal with people then, and would prefer to stay home by myself.

There are a few parts of the world I'd still like to see, but I'm not sure I'll have the chance. I'd like to go to Rome and to Provence. I'd also like to see Canada and one of the countries in Central Africa. I have pictures of these land-scapes in my mind. I'm sure they're wrong, and I'd be surprised if I actually made it to any of them. Nonetheless I'd like to see them someday. But I'm forty now and haven't made it yet, and I don't know whether I'll manage in the next ten years. When I'm old I won't want to travel. Too strenuous.

Now and then I toy with the idea of having a child.

Earlier I wanted to bring a child into the world myself, but always lost courage. Now I'm occasionally seized by the desire to take in an orphaned girl. I picture how my life would change, and I'm convinced I'd be very happy. But in a less sentimental mood I realize that I'm really thinking only of myself. I need the child for my own happiness. I need it for my hopes, to give content to my life. Then my desire seems less benign. I'm afraid it's something like sexual abuse of minors. I'm strong enough to manage alone. I'm not in any crisis. My nerves are in fine shape. (At the hospital I'm considered a sturdy soul; colleagues who are less well disposed call me hard. If I committed suicide, they'd be puzzled. It would be the perfect surprise.) I don't have to abuse a child to replace the love I'm missing. And I hope I don't get myself a dog some day. As a substitute for a substitute.

Still, I know that the desire for a child will keep cropping up occasionally. What's behind it is undoubtedly the longing to surrender myself completely to another person. My lost capacity for loving someone unconditionally. The longing for Katharina, for a child's love, for a kind of friendship that only children are capable of. I miss Katharina very much now. It was twenty-five years ago that I saw her for the last time, and I wish we'd stayed together. We broke apart in the cruel way children do, and both of us probably found it less horrible than it really was. At the time I didn't know that I would never again love another person so unreservedly. The loss hurts me. None of the later separations, from Hinner, from the men who came after him, even from Henry, really upset me. Probably my relationship with them was marked from the beginning by the knowledge that I would lose them someday, or that I might lose them. That good sense made me independent and alone. I'm shrewd, hardened, I can see through everything. Nothing will surprise me anymore. All the catastrophes still hiding ahead won't throw my life into confusion. I'm ready for them. I have enough of what they call life experience. I avoid disappointments. I quickly sense where they might be lurking. I sense them even where they aren't lurking, and sense them so strongly that they finally materialize even there. I'm prepared for everything, I'm armed against everything, nothing will hurt me anymore. I've become invulnerable. Like Siegfried, I have bathed in dragon's blood, and no linden leaf has left a single spot of me unprotected. I'm inside this skin for the duration. I will die inside my invulnerable shell, I'll suffocate with longing for Katharina.

I want to be friends with Katharina again. I want to get out of the thick hide of my fears and mistrusts. I want to see her. I want Katharina back.

My impenetrable skin is my mighty fortress.

I hope I'll always earn enough money so that I'll never have to pinch pennies. My needs are modest, but I intend to satisfy them.

I'm afraid of killing a person or crippling someone for life. Not at the hospital; everything is repairable there. No, I'm afraid of running someone over with the car. I'm not worried for the other person, just for myself. It would be an experience that would change my life decisively, I fear. I don't want that.

Recently I've begun to fear for my photographs. All the drawers and cupboards in my apartment are completely filled. Trees, landscapes, grasses, wagon roads, dead, decaying wood are spilling out at me from all sides. Soulless images of nature that I created, now threatening to drown me. I've already thought of stuffing them into the cupboards in my office, but I'm afraid that Carla would find them and subject me to an interrogation. More and more I have the feeling that I'm wounding the landscape with my ridiculous little pictures. They're fragments that don't capture anything. They lack a horizon, they can't wilt or decay, and thus they also lack hope. Nevertheless, I won't stop making them. I'm afraid to give it up. It does a lot for me; it helps me cope with my problems. I'll go on filling boxes and cupboards with photos. And in twenty or thirty years, when the building superintendent breaks down my door, he'll have one more problem. Let him burn the pictures; for now, I still need them.

A few days after Henry's funeral Herr Krämer came to see me. He brought me the broad-brimmed felt hat that Henry handed him before he was killed. Herr Krämer thought I had more right to the hat than he did. I thanked him. I didn't ask him to sit down, and I didn't offer him anything. After he left, I threw the hat down the garbage chute. I didn't want to keep it even for a minute. I didn't know how long I'd have the courage to throw it away. I can't have my little apartment filling up with old hats.

In the summer I went to the ocean as usual. I visited Fred and Maria again, and everything was like it was before.

I was hoping to see the beautiful girl I met when I was there with Henry last year. She really was beautiful. She gave me something when we said good-bye. This year she wasn't there, and Fred and Maria didn't remember her. I regretted not finding her, but somehow I didn't care. She wasn't at all like Katharina.

I'm fine. Today Mother called, and I promised to visit her soon. Everything's great, I told her.

I'm back to normal. I'm pretty well liked. I have a boy-friend again. I can always pull myself together, it's not hard. I have plans. I like working at the hospital. I sleep well, I don't have nightmares. In February I'm getting a new car. I look younger than I am. I have a hairdresser who takes me without an appointment, a butcher who gives me preferential treatment, a seamstress who has an eye for my style. I have an excellent gynecologist; after all, I'm a col-league. And if it ever came to it, I'd be taken to a first-class institution, the best possible; after all, I'd still be a colleague. I'm satisfied with my apartment. My complexion is good. I can afford the things I enjoy. I'm healthy. I've achieved everything I could achieve. I can't think of any-thing I lack. I've made it. I'm fine.

The End.

A B O U T   T H E   A U T H O R

Christoph Hein, at 44, is one of East Germany's most not-
able literary figures. Poet, playwright, novelist, he has won
the Heinrich Mann Prize, East Germany's most coveted
literary award, and has been widely recognized for his writ-
ings throughout the world. *The Distant Lover* has been translated into seventeen languages; it is the first of Hein's works
to appear in English.

PANTHEON MODERN WRITERS ORIGINALS

THE VICE-CONSUL

by Marguerite Duras, translated from the French by Eileen Ellenbogen

The first American edition ever of the "masterful novel" (*Chicago Tribune*) that Duras considers her best—a tale of passion and desperation set in India and Southeast Asia.

0-394-75026-8

MAPS

by Nuruddin Farah

The unforgettable story of one man's coming of age in the turmoil of modern Africa, by "one of the finest contemporary African writers" (Salman Rushdie).

0-394-75548-0

NELLY'S VERSION

by Eva Figes

An ingenious thriller of identity by the author of *Waking* and *The Seven Ages*.

"A taunting, captivating novel."—*Times Literary Supplement*

0-679-72035-9

DREAMING JUNGLES

by Michel Rio, translated from the French by William Carlson

"A subtle philosophical excursion embodied in a story of travel and adventure...it succeeds extremely well."—*New York Times Book Review*

0-394-75035-7

BURNING PATIENCE

by Antonio Skármeta, translated from the Spanish by Katherine Silver

A charming story about the friendship that develops between Pablo Neruda, Latin America's greatest poet, and the postman who stops to receive his advice about love.

"The mix of the fictional and the real is masterful, and...gives the book its special appeal and brilliance."—*Christian Science Monitor*

0-394-75033-0

THE SHOOTING GALLERY

by Yūko Tsushima, compiled and translated from the Japanese by Geraldine Harcourt

Eight stories about modern Japanese women by "a subtle, surprising, elegant writer who courageously tells unexpected truths." (Margaret Drabble).

0-394-75743-2

YOU CAN'T GET LOST IN CAPE TOWN

by Zoë Wicomb

A "superb first collection" (*New York Times Book Review*) of stories about a young black woman's upbringing in South Africa.

0-394-75309-7

ALSO FROM THE PANTHEON MODERN WRITERS SERIES

A PAINTER OF OUR TIME

by John Berger

John Berger's artistic detective novel, a complex and powerful portrait of an artist at odds with his time.

"Fresh and inventive."—*New York Times*

0-679-72271-8

PIG EARTH

(the first volume of the projected trilogy *Into Their Labors*)

by John Berger

An exquisite fictional portrait of life in a small peasant village in the French Alps.

"Lovely, lyrical, haunting…a masterpiece."—Todd Gitlin, *New Republic*

"A work of art."—*Washington Post*

0-394-75739-4

ONCE IN EUROPA

(the second volume of the projected trilogy *Into Their Labors*)

by John Berger

A linked series of love stories, set among the peasants of Alpine France.

"Berger is one of our most gifted and imaginative contemporary writers [and] *Once in Europa* contains what may be his best writing to date."

—*New York Times Book Review*

"Marvelous stories."—Angela Carter, *Washington Post Book World*

0-394-75164-7

THE MARRIAGE SCENARIOS

by Ingmar Bergman, translated from the Swedish by Alan Blair

The film scripts for *Scenes from a Marriage*, *Autumn Sonata*, and *Face to Face*.

"A terrifically moving piece of writing."—*Los Angeles Times*

0-679-72032-4

ALL FIRES THE FIRE AND OTHER STORIES

by Julio Cortázar, translated from the Spanish by Suzanne Jill Levine

"One of the most adventurous and rewarding collections since the publication of Cortázar's own *Blow-Up*."—*Los Angeles Times*

0-394-75358-5

BLOW-UP AND OTHER STORIES

by Julio Cortázar, translated from the Spanish by Paul Blackburn

A celebrated masterpiece: fifteen eerie and brilliant short stories.

"A splendid collection."—*New Yorker*

0-394-72881-5

THE LEOPARD
by Giuseppe di Lampedusa, translated from the Italian by Archibald Colquhoun
The world-renowned novel of a Sicilian prince in the turbulent Italy of the 1860s.
"The genius of its author and the thrill it gives the reader are probably for all time."
— *New York Times Book Review*
0-394-74949-9

L'AMANTE ANGLAISE
by Marguerite Duras, translated from the French by Barbara Bray
A gripping novel about a savage murder in small-town France.
"Astonishing... a small gem."—Lynne Sharon Schwartz
0-394-75022-5

BLUE EYES, BLACK HAIR
by Marguerite Duras, translated from the French by Barbara Bray
"A novel of erotic obsession, appropriately obsessive in tone."
— *Washington Post Book World*
0-679-72280-7

EMILY L.
by Marguerite Duras, translated from the French by Barbara Bray
"*Emily L.* is a gem." — *Los Angeles Times*
0-394-57233-5

THE RAVISHING OF LOL STEIN
by Marguerite Duras, translated from the French by Richard Seaver
"Brilliant... shoots vertical shafts down into the dark morass of human love."
— *New York Times Book Review*
0-394-74304-0

THE SAILOR FROM GIBRALTAR
by Marguerite Duras, translated from the French by Barbara Bray
By the author of *The Lover*, "a haunting tale of strange and random passion"
(*New York Times Book Review*).
0-394-74451-9

THE WAR: A MEMOIR
by Marguerite Duras, translated from the French by Barbara Bray
"Autobiographical narrative of the highest order."—Philip Roth

"This meditation on the horrors of World War II [is] a complex and extraordinary book."
— Francine du Plessix Gray, *New York Times Book Review*
0-394-75039-X

A GUARD WITHIN
by Sarah Ferguson

The story of a young woman's heroic struggle to recover from a harrowing emotional breakdown.

"Overwhelming."—*New York Times Book Review*

"A stunning and heroic achievement—reminds one of Sylvia Plath's last poems."
—*Chicago Sun-Times*

0-394-75834-X

TRUST
by Mary Flanagan

An "excellent first novel" (*Times*, London) set in London's bohemian art world.

"The writer whose work I kept thinking of as I read this...fine first novel...was E. M. Forster."—Calvin Tomkins, *New York Times Book Review*

0-679-72281-5

NAPLES '44
by Norman Lewis

A young British intelligence officer's journal of his year in Allied-occupied Naples.

"An immensely gripping experience...a marvelous book."—S. J. Perelman

0-394-72300-7

THE ASSAULT
by Harry Mulisch, translated from the Dutch by Claire Nicolas White

The story of a Nazi atrocity in Occupied Holland and its impact on the life of one survivor.

"Brilliant...stunningly rendered."—John Updike

0-394-74420-9

YOUNG TÖRLESS
by Robert Musil, translated from the German by Eithne Williams and Ernst Kaiser

A classic novel by the author of *The Man Without Qualities*, about students at an Austrian military academy and their brutality to one another.

"An illumination of the dark places of the heart."—*Washington Post*

0-394-71015-0

THE WAR DIARIES: NOVEMBER 1939-MARCH 1940
by Jean-Paul Sartre, translated from the French by Quintin Hoare

Sartre's only surviving diaries: an intimate look at his life and thought at the beginning of World War II.

"An extraordinary book."—Alfred Kazin, *Philadelphia Inquirer*

0-394-74422-5

Ask at your local bookstore for other Pantheon Modern Writers titles.